Mistletoe Tales

A D Fitzgerald

2020

For the families now and those who have gone
before, the memory of everyday magic.

Cover Art:
Mistletoe Tales
Becky Salter

Mistletoe Tales

Contents

Prologue - By Balder's Blood

The early morning mist slowly cleared from the plain of Idavoll, the meeting place of the Aesir. The rising sun slowly warming the fertile soils of Asgard, nestled high in the branches of Yggdrasil, the World Tree. Through those dwindling mists crept Loki, a mischievous grin spread across his face. His cloak hung open and tucked in his belt a small silver sickle glinted in the early morning light.

He halted as he approached the oak trees that marked the edge of the plain, carefully transforming his wicked grin into a gentler smile. Once he felt prepared he called out, his voice carefully soft and warm. "Good Morrow sweet Mistletoe. Art thou awake?" He paused, listening to the spirits of the plants that blossomed amongst the boughs of the mighty oaks.

"Good Morrow, Loki. I am. The gentle dawn has delightfully warmed me from the tips of my leaves into my roots." The voice of the plant's spirit came to Loki's mind through the soft swishing of the leaves.

"Ah, gentle Mistletoe. It is indeed a glorious morning and I am pleased that I have not disturbed your rest. It is most auspicious. Last night I had a vision that filled my heart with joy and wonder. The dream planted the seed of an idea which brought me abroad at this early hour. I have a mission in which thou art the most important part.

1

This is why I most humbly beg thy favour. There is a small task that requires thy help, if thou willst.

Every day the Gods play and poor blind Hoder cannot join in their games. That is unless thou lend thy aid, so that I might use some of thee to make a tool that he can wield. I only ask as thou art so light, and kindly.

Oh, most lovely Mistletoe willst thou aid in my plan?" Loki paused allowing the mistletoe's spirit time to consider his vague request and the emotional tone of his appeal. The silence he left was interrupted by the voice of another spirit, deeper than the Mistletoe's.

"Listen not to the trickster. His words are too glib. I fear that this is not all it seems." The Oak's warning resonated slowly through its trunk. The spirit was sleepy and hard to stir at this early hour, but its greater wisdom warned it that something sinister was afoot. Loki gestured quickly using a trick of his magic to subdue the spirit back to sleep. As the spell took hold a couple of green leaves fell from its branches.

"Heed not grumpy old Oak. He is just jealous that I am coming to thee for aid, rather than him. It is only thy aid that will serve in this task. I would have asked him, but he is too stout. If thou help us Hoder can play with Balder after a lifetime of being denied that joy." Loki's tone became entreating, the faint glimmer of a tear appeared to creep from the corner of his eye.

"Balder? And Hoder? They want to play

together? The Gods of Light and Dark at play would be so much fun! The dancing of the dappled shadows that sometimes entrances me would be nothing in comparison. But Loki, I am so small. I don't know what help I canst give. Thy words and Hoder's plight move me so whate'er I can do I will. I give my aid freely!" Loki grinned broadly again at that promise and removed the sickle from his belt. His keen eyes roved over the plant assessing the best place to cut.

"I need but a part of thee to shape the tool for the game. I promise to not take more than I need, and I will be quick. Canst thou be brave and affirm that thou giv'st me willingly what I seek?" Loki raised his empty hand and gently stroked the nearest leaves of the trembling plant.

"Frigg was here a moon or so ago, on some important business, but she told me I was too young to participate. None of the others would tell me what it was about, but I am happy that I am able to help you in this!" The nervous trembling of the spirit of the Mistletoe changed to joy. "I affirm my consent. Cut quickly Loki and I will bear the pain; it is a small sacrifice to make for such a noble endeavour."

"I thank thee and so to work!" Without any further conversation Loki selected the longest branches he could see and quickly cut them from the plant. The plant's spirit mourned the harm it had permitted but it bid farewell to the bundle of cut branches.

3

"Farewell Loki, and that part of me I have surrendered. The knowledge that I will play a role in the games that will unite the two brothers fills me with such joy. Go safely." The spirit retreated to focus on healing the permitted wound. In Loki's hand the severed portion of the Mistletoe spirit stayed in shocked silence.

Quickly bundling the cutting into his cloak Loki retreated to a nearby shelter where he had established a workshop. Warding himself from sight and using his hands and his magic he bent the substance of the mistletoe to his will. Under his efforts it slowly began transforming into a beautifully balanced spear.

As the sun crept towards its zenith, he wiped the sweat from his brow and marvelled at what he had produced, it was spectacular. Aware that his plan needed to unfold slowly he reluctantly enchanted it to be invisible and bound it to his back.

Confident in the concealment charm ready for the next stage he began his journey to find the other Aesir. They were due to be at Balder's home, Breiðablik. The kindly god of light's hall was made of gleaming white stone and the roof was a crystal prism. The early afternoon sun making the entire hall glow and dance with mini versions of Bifröst. Loki's heart was gnawed with the envy that the beauty of this hall inspired. Watching the gods and goddesses blithely enjoying themselves whilst he knew that he was only barely tolerated dripped

4

poison into his heart. This growing bitterness renewed his resolution to sow new discord amongst them.

"It is such a beautiful day brothers and sisters! How shall we spend it?" Loki asked casually tossing the seeds from his apple one by one into the fire pit. Each morsel disappearing with a tiny conflagration when it hit the magical miniature sun that Balder had placed there. "Shall we ride? Mayhaps visit another realm? See if there is a revel in Alfheim that we can join?

I feel quite sure that I shall die of boredom if I continue hitting this target that doesn't move." He carefully kept his eyes fixed on the fiery sphere. His ears keenly listening to the response from the others. He knew that Thor was still saddle sore from a prank he had played on him the previous day.

"I have no spirit for a ride, it is too good a day, but mayhap we can increase our sport by getting a better target!" Thor quickly opined to the room, silencing the few murmurs of agreement that had begun to surface. "Balder! Willst ye give us a better challenge? A moving target this time?" Thor threw a half-gnawed meat bone at his brother and watched it harmlessly bounce away from his shoulder.

"Oh, a challenge ye seek, is it?" Balder responded. As he stood his blonde hair rippled in the light glowing like a ripe cornfield. "I think I can provide the sport that ye seek! None shall say they found the host of Breiðablik wanting when they sought joy and diversion. Let us to the gardens!" The majority of the gods of Asgard, laughing and joking, rose from the table and left the hall, eager to begin the game.

Loki held back and approached Hoder who was still sitting alone at the table savouring his horn of mead. His natural aura of darkness more marked in the vibrant atmosphere of his brother's home. "Come my friend. I think it is most unfair that our brother Thor has once more dictated a revel that excludes thee. My heart is moved in sympathy. However noble Hoder come with me as I feel inspired that we might be able to find a way to make today one that will be remembered as very special!" After some momentary doubt Hoder agreed and Loki took his arm and guided him out of the hall. His gentle whisper allying his blind brother's suspicions and the faint stirring of hope diminishing Hoder's natural gloom. The words of brotherly sympathy touching the blind god's reticent heart.

As they exited the hall Loki could see that Balder had already taken his position at the far end of the field. He had divested himself of his jerkin, and his shirt had fallen open in the warm afternoon air. Soon Balder was jumping around and cartwheeling back and forth as the many weapons and missiles thrown by his siblings harmlessly bounced off him. The general merriment filled the air with laughter and smiles. Loki began relating to Hoder all that was happening, describing the joy on the faces of their siblings at being part of the sport. And carefully pointing out how each weapon was leaving not a scratch on his brother's flesh. Balder's part in the sport included goading them to try harder.

"Come now Aesir! This is paltry work, more strength to thy blows!" The good god teased them. He was confident in the immunity granted to him by his mother, Frigg's compact with the things of the world to do him no harm. Hanging back with Hoder at the rear of crowd Loki was now sure that none were paying attention to them as the game was in full flow.

"Hoder! Thou knowst I said I was moved by thy plight and I had an idea. Now is the time to reveal it. I have made thee a present!" Unweaving the illusion of invisibility from the spear he removed it from his back and carefully placed it in the Hoder's waiting hands. "Thou canst finally participate. I have always thought it unfair that thou hast never had a turn at this sport! Come. This spear is light and should aim true. I made it to go where the thrower wishes. Feel that balance and the heft. It will be a merry missile to add to the fun. I will even guidest thy hand! Dost thou agree?" Loki's smile was genuine but Hoder could not see the glint of malice that danced in his eyes.

"Guide me well Loki! It has been too long

that I have been deprived of the joy of participating in this game! Ho there Brother! Balder! Let us see how this fares! Now Loki, now!" Hoder and Loki's conjoined hands sent the spear sailing true through the air above the heads of the sportive Aesir.

Balder froze when Hoder's voice called him. His surprise at hearing his brother saying he would participate rooting him to the spot. It was with a gentle smile that he watched the descending arc of the spear and even steadied his stance as he welcomed the impact. It did not deviate. It struck true and stood proud from his chest. The smile faded into shock as he realised that he was mortally injured. A flood of prophetic nightmares that had haunted him until Frigg's intervention returned as he fell. He saw the same shock echoed in the eyes of his family standing before him. This was the last thing he saw. The last echoes of their laughter dying with him as he hit the ground.

Into that painful silence that seemed to last for an age Frigg screamed. Her beautiful face twisted with the pain of seeing her son struck down as in her nightmares. She fled to her fallen child. The other gods turned to look behind to see whence the spear had sprung and their eyes fixed on Hoder. Standing there alone. His hands feeling fruitlessly for the presence of his trickster brother. "Loki? What has happened? What is amiss? Why dost my mother cry so?" Frey and Bragi went to him and steadied his reaching hands.

Summoned by the screams Eir, the healer, entered the garden. She hurried to where Frigg was weeping over Balder's body, cradling his head in her lap. Frigg gently stroked his forehead and smoothed his hair as if he were a fretful infant. Eir's quick assessment ended with tears falling from her eyes. Although his body was still warm his essence had flown, the glow of life was fading from his body. Odin came and stood by Frigg and silently placed a gentle hand on her shoulder.

Vengeful Vidar joined the small group, his eyes ablaze with righteous rage. Swiftly pulling the spear from his fallen half-brother his fist clenched tight around the supple shaft. His anger burning through his normal silence. The low intensity of his voice as he rebuked the plant was even more chilling than a shout. "Name thyself! Before I punish thee I willst hear thy name. Speak oh treacherous Spirit! Oath-breaker I name thee."

"I am of the Mistletoe." The shattered shard of spirit whispered back. The shame and shock at the its role in Balder's death tormenting it even whilst it was still adjusting to the form Loki had forced upon it.

"And so shall thee perish. Thou took the life of Balder against all bargains made by Frigg. As thou stand untrue to thy oath, thou must pay the price. Only death can pay for life." Vidar began to summon his power to smite the mistletoe and to take his vengeance on to all its kind. As he was

9

about to release his vengeance a soft white hand appeared on his and he froze. The power of the goddess held him fast.

"Thou art nearly right, strong Vidar. However, thou art mistook. I made no bargain with the mistletoe. No oath was broken in this act, which does reduce the crime. But this murder cannot pass without amends being made. There is a still a price to be paid. I will take thy words Vidar and say the opposite is more true. Only life can pay for death.

Balder has been taken from us, we are diminished by that. His goodness has been taken from the world. This mistletoe must now take up a share of that burden. I have lost my son, therefore I name the blood price. The blood which even now seeps into your being. Mistletoe, thou and all that share thy spirit, must bring what joy and peace thou canst. From now, for ever. I command that thee use the power that thou have to achieve these ends. And to seal this command I share my tears with ye lest ye forget the sorrow that this day thou hast wrought." She gently settled Balder's head upon the ground and took the spear from the hands of Vidar, her stepson. Walking away from the grim scene she felt the spear change in her hands as she walked towards the nearby apple trees that sheltered in a sunny spot in her late son's garden. It unfurled itself and returned to the shape it was before Loki's manipulations.

"Though art empowered by the blood of Balder that flows through thee. Bring the joy and the peace that thy complicity in Loki's dark deed hath taken from this world. The author of this scheme will pay another price, I swear it. This is thy share of the burden for all eternity." As Frigg approached the apple tree her tears fell onto the newly reformed branches and they flowed to the ends, condensing into pearl white berries. Taking the branch, she thrust it with all her might into the side of the nearest tree, which gently accepted its burden. The spirit of the Apple having witnessed the death of a god was not willing to refuse the grieving mother and accepted the thrust in silent grief.

"I will take this burden and do what I can. I will grieve my part in this for all time." the spirit of the Mistletoe promised.

The force of that oath sealed in the blood of one god and the tears of another echoed down Yggdrasil. The promise binding all mistletoe to the same penance across all nine worlds. Its innocence lost in the taking of a life, it was now able to enter into such compacts with the gods as it must.

Many moons later, it consented again to being cut at Frigg's behest, when the Ambassador from Alfheim requested a boon for services rendered to the Aesir. The elves mostly keep their own counsel, but they travel through all the worlds of Yggdrasil and the tales of the Mistletoe reach down even to Midgard and the realms of mortal men.

The Lover's Promise

The rain pelted down on the sodden earth
as the faint suggestion of the winter sun set sullenly
behind the hills. The broad valley slowly filled
with the common mixture of mist and darkness
that deterred all but the most determined people
from venturing out. Through this gathering gloom
a small and solitary figure stomped onwards to her
destination, a small oil cloth lined wicker basket
clutched tightly against her body.

It was not a night to be away from the
fireside but needs must. There was a soul crying for
help, or more than one if she was seeing rightly,
and she knew in her bones that time was running
short. The reserves of hope run low in the depths of
winter. Reaching her destination, she was hurriedly
welcomed inside against the dreary night.

Alone in the short corridor that ran through
the centre of Crow Farm cottage Mother Beecham
stamped the heavy clay mud from her boots. The
flagstones underfoot were already well covered, a
sign of simple neglect that added to her feeling that
something was amiss. A few sods on the stone it
may just be, but the echoes of 'and to earth we shall
return' hung in her mind. Her host, Rachel Crow,
had scurried back into the kitchen 'to get the tea'. It
was not just magic that allowed the witch to sense

12

the woman's fear, it was mingled with a sense of desperate need that hung around her like a mist.

Mother Beecham's heavy woollen shawl had become sodden in the long walk from Old Bridge to the Crow steading. She carefully draped it over her arm to set it to dry by the fire. She would be damned if she went back still damp, and doubly damned if she didn't fix the pain that she could feel festering in the house.

She cautiously followed Rachel into the kitchen. Aware that her unannounced visit would likely be a problem with Rachel's husband, Mr Crow. He was known as Mr Crow even to his wife. A man of few words, and even fewer friends, his sour spirit made most fear him. The kitchen which served as parlour, dining room and overspill dairy, in the small cottage was a little haven of calm. The gentle lamp light added to the warmth from the fire, but the atmosphere was a weak illusion created by Rachel to try and soothe her own troubled spirit. Mother Beecham opened her senses wider to determine if she was in luck. Beyond this room, and Rachel's aching heart, she could only detect the source of her premonition of unease, a sharp prickling of an otherworldly presence. She was relieved to find that Mr Crow

13

was definitely away on business, as if he had been home she feared he would have interfered.

"Ah, this is cosy." Mother Beecham said taking the seat that she had been nodded towards as the worried woman bustled around her. With a deft movement Rachel took possession of her guest's shawl and settled it to dry by the fire. Mother Beecham kept her tone light as the slight redness and tightness around Rachel's eye spoke volumes. She let the silence grow. Giving space for the anxious to find their own voice was better than a flood of kindly meant questions.

Keeping a close eye on her host she watched as the tea things were set on the table. Mother Beecham nodded at the generosity when a pot of preserves and a small heel of bread were set on the cloth between them. The practical demands of making the tea kept Rachel moving, her hands completing the habitual actions of a good hostess. Her eyes were the only sign that this was a woman in whom the spark of hope had nearly gone out. The kettle began to sing, the only sound in the room other than the crackle of the fire and the two women's gentle breathing.

The pot filled, the cups set, Rachel finally sat and faced Mother Beecham. It was the first time that she had ever observed her closely and it was the first visit that the old witch had ever paid to her home, but she was a familiar figure nonetheless. Everyone for miles around knew who she was. Mother Beecham, the witch of Old Bridge. No one ever looked at her too closely. It was never done to stare, not unless 'ye wanted to risk the evil eye'. Or at least that was what her sisters had told her as they grew up. The respectful fear, that familiarity of reputed danger. The reverend had recently been scoffing at the tales of her powers, claiming it was empty superstition and spite against an old lady. Rachel knew differently, he wasn't from around here, he didn't know the land or the people. Mother Beecham was their witch, and everyone knew that she was not to be trifled with.

Rachel felt that knowledge in her bones, but she was tired of being scared. Mother Beecham was a danger, because she was powerful, but that had never stopped people going to her for help. If they dared. Meddling with things that might otherwise be best left alone. Rachel felt the thorn digging into her heart, pretending it wasn't there had nearly worn her out. Mr Crow's simple instruction to tell no one had been made weeks back. Her final appeal had led to him muttering "T'aint natural." and she saw the darkening in his eyes that made

15

Rachel freeze to her bones and comply. But her fear of him and the fears of her childhood were lessening as another fear grew which now took over her mind. The fear of losing her son. As full grown as he was now, he was still her little boy and seeing him fading from life was more than she could bear. As a mother she had to put aside the fears of fairy tales, and Mr Crow was away to Middleton for the night. She had this one opportunity. The knowledge that she had a choice passed through her like a chill wind and made her shudder.

Looking at the witch she could see she was just another woman. The same as her, more grey hair, more lines, a few fewer teeth but beyond the stories they were the same. Skin, blood and bone. The only difference was the eyes. The witch's eyes burned into her. To try and distract herself from that feeling of being peeled away to her very core, Rachel reached for the tea and nearly sent everything flying from the table. Her hands were shaking and she settled them on the pot to steady herself. Then she felt the warm hands of the old woman covering hers. They felt very soothing.

"Such a to do. Here let me." Mother Beecham gently took the pot from her host's failing grip. "I already am called mother so I might as well act the part too." She chuckled at her own joke and Rachel felt a weak smile touch her own lips. She pulled a handkerchief from her sleeve and dabbed at her eyes.

"Thank thee." She managed to murmur. Had the moment passed? Was it too late? Her thoughts began to race. She hadn't said anything, did she need to? Would Mother Beecham just know what was wrong? Why had she come here tonight? The questions filled her head but her tongue felt like it turned to stone in her mouth. Mother Beecham sipped her tea and eventually filled the silence.

"I heard today from Abel Smith that no one had seen neither hide nor hair of thy Adam since the funeral. Not even at Mass for Christmas, and that was near a week past. I says to myself, I says, what can be ailing that young man?" Mother Beecham suspected she knew but wanted to hear what would be said. On the way over she had been thinking on him, the vision of him shrouded in darkness had been her sign. Adam was a well kennt face to her, he was a bonny lad, kind to everyone. Once last winter, when the ice had been black and treacherous, she had fallen on the main street of the village. The first she had seen from the

17

ground was his face bending over, concern in his gentle eyes. He had given a warm hand and strong arm to see her safely back to her cottage when she had been ready to be put back on her feet. A kindness is never forgotten by a witch.

Mother Beecham observed Rachel closely; her hands were no longer shaking. She could sense the fear and hopelessness was slowly transforming in this woman, just a little more priming and the tale would come freely.

"And it being a bad time for sicknesses this winter and the such I thought to myself, I thought might it not be a kindness to visit in upon the young man and see if I can be a help." She could tell that her words had struck home. Rachel nodded softly and dabbed at her eyes again.

"Aye, it would be a kindness. It has been so terrible." Rachel finally managed to speak, her voice betraying the emotions that she was trying to keep in check. Mother Beecham nodded and sipped her tea, allowing the silence to be filled by the tale of woe that Rachel was now able to share.

Mother Beecham sat and listened to her tell of the suffering and worry that had taken Adam like a fiend when he had first learnt of Iain's illness. His best friend, as close as brothers, Adam had taken it so bad. Raged against it as if shouting could change the fates. Until that was, the funeral. Then he went quiet and it was like they had put him in the ground too.

Mother Beecham watched Rachel pause and make the small hand gesture to avert the ill luck of what she had said. She recalled that she had been turned away by Iain's family who wanted no part of her witchcraft in their house. The priest had been called and was praying over him, but not even a word of medicine was allowed. She held her tongue, this was not the time to air her feelings, it was Rachel's time. She would only help where she was wanted, and past battles are never won by dwelling on them after they are over. The current one was where she was needed.

Mother Beecham let the mother cry out her fears. They were the canker that was eating at her heart, near as bad as that which had taken young Iain. Holding Rachel's hand she listened and consoled her the best she could. This was the easier part of tonight's work. She still had to save the young man who might be too far gone for her skill. She could feel the tide in the house, it was on the turn and if she wasn't swift he may go with the ebb. Especially if he was being encouraged to let go.

"Now, Rachel, I have heard thee and I think that I can help, so it's time for me to see Adam. Show me the way please." Mother Beecham gathered herself and collected her basket from the bench in the hallway as they headed up the narrow wooden stairs. Rachel led the way with a small lamp, the top of the stairs ending in two small wooden doors.

Pushing open the right-hand door Rachel's lamp cast light onto a scene of misery. Night had now fully fallen but there was a deeper darkness within this room. On the small cot bed, the figure of the young man lay in his nightshirt. It was soiled with sweat amidst a tangle of blankets and sheets. His long back curled against them as he hugged his knees tight to his body and his bare feet protruding from the mess. His toes and the fingers of his hands curled unnaturally tight as if trying to both hold himself in and brace himself against the air. The atmosphere was heavy with the odour of self-neglect and misery.

Mother Beecham waved her hand to pre-emptively silence Rachel; she could sense the automatic apology coming unbidden to the mother's lips. This was far from her first sickbed and this was far from the worse sight that she had seen over her long years. Taking a taper from the bedside shelf she lit the bedside lamp from the one Rachel carried and allowed the light to settle.

"Leave us now." Mother Beecham instructed Rachel. Her voice was quiet but firm. The mother paused, torn between anguish at the sight of her son in such pain and the belief that Mother Beecham could help and should be obeyed. A brief glance from Mother Beecham spurred her into movement. Latching the door behind her she retreated to the sanctuary of the kitchen.

Waiting as she listened to the footsteps fade downstairs Mother Beecham studied her patient. His unruly red hair and pale skin gave him an air of innocence. While she reckoned most people were still children measured against her life, he looked even more childlike in his illness. He was however old enough to be walking out. Some of his age had already jumped the broom a year past and were on their way to making their own little ones. But not this one. Watching him now she sensed that he had a harder path to walk. Harder now than he had thought it would be.

Listening to his breathing she could tell he was awake. He just didn't want to be. In the still of the bedroom the sound of the rain was louder, the thin window and shutter a scant barrier against the natural forces at play outside. She settled herself and her basket on the edge of the bed.

"So, it has been a rough winter young Adam. And here ye are abed. Best place for anyone in this weather I vouch, but possibly good to rise come the morrow. It is nigh on the new year, and time to see things afresh." Mother Beecham kept her voice soft but with a hint of gentle teasing.

The silence that greeted this did not surprise her. If it only took some mild jollity to cure the young man this would not have been a problem that required her skills. Jolly was not the normal description that people applied to Mother Beecham, but witches do what they must. As the silence continued she closed her eyes and opened her heart. She knew that something was wrong, it had called out to her across the miles but it was not as she expected. She had thought that at best the sorrow was a shroud on his senses but there was no such sign. Worse would have been if a strong net of attachment was dragging him away from the world, with another pulling the rope. Instead it was almost like he wasn't there. She delved deeper and realised how far it had gone. The sorrow was woven throughout his body. It was becoming his being. His heart was becoming as cold as the ice which the rain had melted and would return again

once the clouds cleared. The ice he wouldn't live to
see unless she melted that which had taken root
within him. He was in his own thrall and not being
lured away as she had feared, but that may still be
the best tool to reach him. His lost friend.

"Now Adam. I know ye miss him, but what
would Iain say if he saw ye like this?" Mother
Beecham saw his body tense and shudder when
she said the name. He went limp, the tightness in
his body gone. Mother Beecham feared for a
moment he had managed to leave already by sheer
force of will. She quickly checked and realised that
it was only the next stage of his grief, he was
slipping further away.

She was going to have to act quickly, he was
already further gone than she had thought possible
this quickly. The young could be so headstrong.
Pulling a small canvas sack from her basket she
scattered some salt around them in a circle.
Readying the space for the next challenge. There
was no balm that she could make, but there might
be one that she could bring. She was going to do a
summoning rather than a banishment.

Reaching deeper into the basket she pulled
out a bundle of white silk tied with a golden
ribbon. As she unwrapped it she prepared herself
for what was to come next. At her age one looks on

23

the deceased with a more tightly mingled sense of compassion and curiosity. A soul would soon be on their side of the veil, this meant it was approached with more caution than when you were young.

The layers of silk parted to reveal the hints of golden green within, the berries still white despite their age. Her mistletoe wand. Woven together from multiple cuttings, the sprays formed a sturdy but short wand. Bound by threads of red and green still just visible but slowly losing their distinctness with age. The leaves were allowed to escape the structure at times to nestle the berries and to show the nature of the plant. Mother Beecham opened herself to the power imbued in the wand. She said his name and opened her eyes again. She surveyed the shadows in the small room.

"There thou art alright. I thought that thee might be here. Or nearby at least." She calmly looked up and down the spirit of the recently departed Iain McDonald. Even in the low light of the room she could see that his dark hair was as curly and unruly as it had been in life. He was mostly there, but transparent enough that even without her magic Mother Beecham would have been able to tell that he was not of this world.

"Mother Beecham! Ye can see me? Help him. I beg ye!" the voice was the same, strong but still holding the hesitant timbre of youth. No passing years would now change that for him. His face was contorted with anguish. But clearly not for himself.

"Aye, I see thee. Iain McDonald and thou cannot pass my circle and nor canst thou cross me, this night or ever. I command here and I would speak with thee." She had changed her tone to one of command. More than one tale she had heard of the lost soul who was too scared to pass on alone she had braced her for a struggle to free their grip on a loved one in this world. But seeing the shape of Adam's grief and hearing him speak she now knew that this was not the case. His first words had been to ask for help for Adam not for himself. The stories warned of jealous connections to life and anger at the injustice of lost years. This was not that.

"I'd ne'er cross thee. Not this night, nor ever. Dead I may be, but fool I ain't. I see more clear now than I had. I'm sorry for aught I did that harmed ye in life. My humour was ill done but I beg hold that not 'gainst me. I beg ye, help him. He isn't to die. Stop him." The spirit came to the edge of the salt circle and he fell to his knees. The salt glowed faintly where the spectral figure pushed gently against the barrier. The air above the circle shimmering silver at the points of contact. The magical wall holding firm.

"Now stop that lad. I hold little account of fools being about foolishness. And none are more foolish than young men are. So, I let it go. Least said, soonest mended. I hear thy plea. I hear it clear. Ye beg not for thyself, which is right surprising given thy circumstance. But thou plead'st help for thy friend. It commends ye well, right well indeed. Thy heart is good, albeit that it has stopped beating. And there is those for whom I can't say as much whose blood still flows. Fret not I will hear thee out and do what I can to help."

The restless shade of the departed young man returned to its feet. Pacing back and forth in the small bedroom, the light and shadow played tricks making him seem at turns more substantial or nearly invisible. Mother Beecham looked over her shoulder, the figure on the bed had become as clenched as a fist once more. The tension filled his body. She could almost feel the anger as a heat within him. A tight smile danced across her old lips. That anger might either melt his grief or flare and turn him to ash, only time would tell which.

She had to play the whole game now she had started. She returned her attention to the anxious ghost.

"I love him Mother Beecham, and he me. Ye know that? I can say it the now. I told him, but no other knew it. We hid. But oh, it was sweet. Ye needs to know. I care not anymore, but I can see thy heart is not turned against me as I say it. We were so feart that anyone who knew would shame us. That they would take us before the priest or make cruel sport of our love. He made my days so sweet and now I feel his heart break. I see him turn as grey as the ash in the hearth and he pines for me. I can't let him join me now. He has to live. Make him live Mother Beecham.

Ye know how people are. I harkened to that Priest his favourite phrase "all is sin". His prayers as I lay choking in my bed felt like empty words. He demanded that I confess all my faults before he would aid me, and I held back the words that I knew would only make him more angry. He needled me as if he knew that I refused to unburden my soul to him. That there was a secret that I held safe in my heart even as I felt it falter. For it was love and how can love be sin? How can happiness be sin? Adam's smile made the heart in me race, and to see him smile back made it break

27

until it was whole again. I think I see it more now. The priest said that sin comes from the Latin for guilt, he held forth as ye should feel guilty for doing wrong, as if that were proof and the whole pudding.

But I cry nay! Guilt and shame come from others, our love was not wrong in our ain eyes. But without me Adam sickens as he only sees the gap where I should be and feels the shame that others give him for his grief. He thinks that without me he has nae hope. I grieve that I was taken from him, but this isnae his time. His life is my hope and I want to see him carry our love with him rather than allow it to drag him to an early grave." Iain stopped and fell again to his knees, pressing his hands on the invisible barrier that kept him apart from his love. The witch simply nodded as his words struck deep.

"Aye. Aye, I hear thee clear. Thy passion young Iain does thee credit. Dear heart that thou hast, it seest clear with love, not blinded as others would have us think comes from such passions. Thou hast the right of it, both of the priest and of Adam here now what can ...." Mother Beecham's response was cut off by the cry of rage that came from beside her.

"Foul hag, crazy old biddy, how can ye sit there and speak as if Iain is here? It makes a mockery of my grief. I saw his eyes close for the last time near a month gone, and where were ye then? Cowed and kept at bay by that cruel priest who muttered pointlessly by his bedside and kept me from speaking true of my heart as he left me. The dark earth has eaten his bones and I will join him soon. Ye come here unbidden and act some mummers play as if I were I child to be so fooled. And put at peace as easy as if I were a boy with a broken toy. I saw him, go. I saw... I saw him end. And that is all of it, I must end too.

Hate me if ye want but I loved him. Friend thee called him, but nay he was more to me than that, he was my heart, my love, and my husband in all but Christian rite. I am as good as gone since he is no more. And ye come in the night to mock me with this sham, I will none of it. Begone! Get thee gone. Leave! I would just wait it out and summon the reaper to me by my dark prayers. The sin in me is deep and will not be uprooted, so I pray for damnation and the swift end that is a blessed release that I may gaze upon him again. Even if that is lit by the fires of hell. Now begone I say!"

Lethargic from his self-imposed death watch he reached for Mother Beecham to try and force her from the bed. Grasping her shoulder he began to heave against her, but was shocked to find despite his rage and youthful strength that she was as firmly planted as the foundations of the house.

As quick as a snake she took hold of one of his wrists. The old hands strong and steady she guided his hand to join her own which was grasping the wand. As he touched it he froze. The witch's power, the magic of the mistletoe and his own grief combined to open his sight more clearly than even Mother Beecham's own skilled clairvoyance. He was so still that she feared his heart had shattered for true upon the shock of the revelation. She breathed her own small sigh of relief when she felt him shudder and begin to sob.

"Hush, hush now my dearest." Iain crooned to his mourning lover. "I am here, thou seest it right. Good Mother Beecham wasn't playing thee for a fool, she has just opened thy eyes. She knows it, she knows us, our secret was shared by us both and I trust her. I thank her for her pains. Our time is short, the love betwixt us is strong, but I cannot bide here for much longer. Nay, don't look as if in haste to join me. That is why I remained so close for so long, not to ease thee into joining me in the dark valley but to try and stay thy hand. I wished to see thee smile one more time." Iain now pressed both his hands on the boundary made by the magic circle, the glow spreading out from them delineating the barrier as a spider's web of dancing light.

Standing abruptly Adam dragged Mother Beecham from her seat, passion succeeding where his rage had been futile. She retained her steely grip on both the mistletoe wand and her patient. It took all her determination to stay his progress as he was intent on crossing outside of the protection of the thin barrier of the magic circle.

"Stay. While I trust this is the shade of Iain and not a deception, we are safest within the circle whilst we commune across the veil." Adam looked upon her the disbelief etched on his features that she could contemplate keeping him from being with his love.

"I care not for safe! I would be with him before the sun rises. And ye are surely not afeard of that veil which thou dally so much with and draws so nigh to thy person that it must serve as the extra shawl to thy body." Mother Beecham hid how these words stung, harsh truth cuts deeper than kind lies.

"Fie on thee my love. How canst thou be so cruel? I know thou art headstrong, but I am not here to take thee with me. I did rather bide to bid thee the farewell that we were denied. Mother Beecham has done us a kindness that merits better grace than thou art giving. I feel the pain of our loss too, but let it not make thy heart hard.

I would command thee to live. I command thee to love again.

Shake not thy head at this. It is my true wish. I see thy life should be a long one and I wish that thou be happy for all its duration. The burden of thy life cut short is not one that I would carry through the dark valley. It would slow my steps if thou diest for the memory of thy love for me, rather than livest for it.

So live and I beg of thee keep our love as a kernel of joy in thy remaining years. If thou dost not then I would see only the darkness my death had brought rather than the joy that we had shared. Make not thy life bitter with the memory of loss but make it sweet with the remembrance of love."

Mother Beecham held back the tears that came at his words. Adam was unable to find that reserve and slumped against her and he began to cry, the meltwater of his grief bursting forth from the dam he had built inside.

"But I love thee. How can I go on?" Adam managed between the sobs.

"Day by day. From each sunrise to the next. That is the only way. I will always love thee. Thou art a strong man, a good man. Thou willt heal. Thy heart I give back to thee, but for the part I keep made of the memories of the love we shared. Just as thou hold that part of mine. I will wait for thee beyond. Thou spoke of hell and damnation. I get no sense that is what awaits us. While others try and shame us we know the purity of our love is not tainted by such things. I will wait for thee. This I vow to thee. But thou must give me thy bond in turn that thou will make me wait a long time!"

Adam nodded. Mother Beecham remained silent in the face of such love and aware that she was only present to make this conversation possible. Despite her long life she was awed by the passion that she felt between them.

"I make one further condition on that vow. We must seal it with a kiss!" Adam found his voice again, the determination clear. Both the lovers, the living and the dead looked at Mother Beecham. The unspoken question hanging in the intense silence. Would she permit the breaking of the circle?

Carried along by the power of the moment she nodded too. As Adam had said the risks to her were low so if she was wrong, the price of crossing the veil this night would be acceptable. More acceptable than the burden of denying the love between these two tormented souls. Her consent would give them both peace.

She shuffled forward a little and extended her boot to break the line of salt she had made portioning the bed away from the rest of the room.

"Let him kiss me with the kisses of his mouth, for his love is better than wine." Iain spoke as he crossed the broken boundary. He appeared to take on more substance as he drew closer to his lover.

Mother Beecham averted her eyes. She could, through her grasp on the mistletoe wand, feel the exact moment when the two souls connected. Iain's departure was as gentle as a sigh. No banishing required. She turned and embraced the sobbing young man. Her own heart broken by witnessing the strength of the love between them. A love that would carry them on their respective journeys until they were reunited once more.

The Maiden's Dream

Abigail saw the movement from the corner of her eye but kept her head down and pretended she hadn't seen anything. The swift, but not swift enough, movement of her sister, Mary-Agnes', hand pilfering some scraps of greenery from table to apron pocket.

The flickering light of the oil lamps the only illumination as they worked at finishing off the tasks for tomorrow. They had banked the fire earlier than normal to keep the room cool, this would both preserve the altar decorations for the Christening, and also keep the dainties for the post celebration feast fresher.

The deepening chill stiffened their fingers as they delicately tightened the bright ribbons around the last of the sprays of winter flowers and evergreens for the church. The task completed Abigail, the younger of the two, looked around the room satisfied with their evening's work. Her hair was demurely braided as befitted a married woman, her elder sister, still unwed had her hair loosely held back for their work. It constantly threatened to break free and she distractedly tucked one of the errant strands behind her ear. It had often been said by their father, God rest his soul, that it was as unruly as she was.

"Shall we retire to the parlour? Jacob will have a good fire going and we can show Aunt Grace how ye are improving on thy stitching? That last job was right neat, after the first inch or so." Abigail said wiping her hands on her apron and making to extinguish the lamp.

"Nay, I've a weariness on me tonight. And tomorrow will all be awash with such excitement that I must seek my rest." Mary-Agnes' voice had just the right hint of tiredness to not sound a lie, although Abigail suspected that it was not a dreamless sleep that her sister sought.

"Sleep well Sister, I'll see thee before cock crow so we can finish the last tasks. And mind ye that tomorrow morn we expect young Crow too from the dairy." She paused and laughed at herself. "Heh, Crow will be here before the crow! Now there's a thing." Her sister's silence brought her back to herself. "Anyway, he is bringing us that fresh cream and our account is due, so look out my purse from the press if ye are first up." Abigail lightly touched her sister's hair as she passed and extinguished the lamp. Behind her she heard Mary-Agnes' footsteps ascend the stair, As she stepped into the parlour the heat brought a flush to her cheeks.

"Oh! It is a bitter winter." she muttered as she warmed her hands at the fire. "How is the bairn?" She asked taking the swaddled bundle once she was no longer too chilled to fright the child. Aunt Grace had been keeping company with her Jacob and been watching their baby while she worked to prepare for the celebration. With the fire banked the kitchen had become too cold after sundown for either her elderly aunt or her babe in arms. He stirred at her presence and started squirming to be fed. Settling herself by the fire she provided him the breast and relaxed as he sated himself.

"He is a bonny wee thing, not a peep out of him, despite the chill." Grace cooed approvingly while pulling her shawl closer around herself. "It might just be these old bones or this house, but I can feel the fingers of Jack Frost making free with my person in ways that I disapprove of." She surveyed the room as if checking that Mr Frost were in fact not present.

"Oh, so it was Jack Frost that ..." Jacob began his voice dripping with his version of wry humour.

"We will have a warmer house come the morn, once we are making the other part of the christening feast and everyone is gathered. And fret not tonight as Mary-Agnes is up already so the bed will be all the warmer for her turning in early." Abigail interrupted her husband, knowing full well if he finished that sentence in the tone he was using that it would take more than a hearty fire to banish the chill in the room, even with the windows shuttered and curtained.

"Indeed, she is a good girl. Such a shame that she is still unwed while here ye are with thy first born getting christened come the morn. Marrying out of turn, wasn't allowed in my day. But I daresay that it is the way of these things nowadays. I had to wait only on your aunt Norah, and ye know she was so keen that it was a good thing her wedding dress fitted on the day. And come harvest time, with the babe born so large for coming as early as she claimed it must." Grace reached for the teapot and topped off her cup. Jacob and Abigail exchanged a silent look that said all it needed to. Jacob wisely returned to his book.

"Aunt Grace, would ye be so kind as to check over something for me? I was trying a new stitch, well new to me, and it is all of a tangle." Abigail deftly pulled her current work in progress from her craft basket and engaged her aunt in the more neutral topics of threads and fabrics rather than dredging up family history, or rehashing her sister's lack of romantic success. The sermon on that topic she had delivered yesterday to Mary-Agnes herself had been enough for them all.

Upstairs Mary-Agnes had done her best to remain calm while she donned her nightgown. She needed haste so that she was done with her task before Aunt Grace came to bed. She did not want to be interrupted and she had to remember all that the girls at the market had whispered to her. It was a complicated charm that they had passed on. Sally Watson had sworn that Mother Beecham had told her the spell. The sprig under the pillow wasn't even a half of it. Mary-Agnes burned with the shame of needing to keep it secret, being an old maid in her twenties, a good three years older than the others rankled.

She had even kept it from Abigail. How could her sister understand, when she had already found her husband? And even one from a different town. Mary-Agnes had swallowed her pride when the chance came to move with her to the village. It had been to help her sister during her confinement, she had then decided to stay. Her only other choices that she could see were to remain out in the far valley and either die alone or take a chance with some random traveller as there were no prospects in the men who her family worked with or the local farms.

Mary-Agnes had cursed her luck when the fever had kept her home that summer and Abigail had ventured to the Crosstown market in her stead. She felt that her chance had been stolen and she had cried bitterly when Abigail had returned, smiling like the cat who had the cream. She always had had the luck of the devil and having snared herself Jacob that was the final straw. Mary-Agnes wanted her chance, and this was her time, she needed to know what was in store for her.

She had tried the apple peel trick so many times, that she had baked pies for weeks, but not once were their initials that she could decipher. This seemed more trustworthy, and more magical. She took the mistletoe from her apron pocket, sat on the side of her bed and stared at it. What was the ritual again?

Plucking three hairs from her head she slowly began winding the first of them around the stem of the mistletoe. The green smell of the cut plant filling her nostrils. She began to whisper, her voice as low as possible so not to carry to the rest of the house.

"Around thee I bind my hair. I would see true and fair. As I slumber this sprig above, thou willt show me my true love." The candle on her bedside table made dancing shadows as she repeated the spell twice more, each time wrapping a fresh hair around the mistletoe. Cradling the small plant in her hands, her feeling of loss and desperate hope shaping the plea to the universe to give her the message she was waiting for. She needed confirmation that there was a man out there who would love her. That she would have a future beyond her sister's husband's house or back with her mother in their ramshackle isolated cottage.

The first part completed she quickly put her hair into loose plaits for sleeping, her ears carefully attuned to ensure that she was not going to be interrupted by Aunt Grace coming to bed before she had time to complete the last bit of the spell.

She carefully plucked two berries from the sprig of mistletoe and crushed one between the thumb and forefinger fingers, of each hand. The inner flesh of the berry was thick and sticky. She wiped the white substance on the lids of each eye. Muttering quietly "Let me see." She had been told she had to keep her eyes closed once she did this part of the spell until she fell asleep. As she finished she realised that the sprig was not yet under her pillow. Reaching her hand down to collect it she felt her fingers brush it and it span away from her off the eiderdown.

"No!" she suppressed the wail into a heartfelt but breathless keen. Lowering herself slowly to the floor she gently patted around but couldn't feel it. Her heart raced and knew she had to complete the spell. She cracked open one eye and found the sprig inches away from her reaching hand. She quickly gathered it to her chest. Shutting her eye again and prayed that the spell would be forgiving. She shivered as she slipped into the icy sheets either from the cold or from her fear, she couldn't tell which. The flickering light of the single candle she left to guide her aunt to bed played over her tightly closed eyelids.

Burrowing down into the soft mattress she put the mistletoe under her pillow. Her hope and fear kept sleep at bay, and within the confines of her mind she began silently counting sheep. Eventually the darkness behind her eyes rose to welcome her and she slipped into a deep sleep.

Grace's clumsy entrance a while later did not make her stir. The elderly woman looked fondly at her sleeping niece. She was not homely, mayhaps a tad too wide of the face, but that was a family trait. She herself looked similar at that age and it hadn't stopped her from pursuing and winning her own Tommy, God rest him. She quickly slipped from her widow's weeds and into her nightgown. Extinguishing the candle, she climbed into bed, grateful that her niece's body heat had taken the chill from the bed. Soon the darkened room was only filled with the sound of soft breathing and the occasional gentile snore.

Many hours later Mary-Agnes opened her eyes, the last vestiges of the dream still with her, but it was fading. She cried silent tears, her face burning hot with her shame for having ruined the spell. Her vision in the dream had been blurred and confused. All that she had been able to tell of the man in her dreams was his general shape and his hair colour. It was auburn, a coppery red. The oddest part of the dream that lingered had been the nearly overpowering smell of fresh milk.

She slipped from the bed, taking care not to disturb Aunt Grace. The sky was softening from the deep crystal darkness with the early hint of false dawn. The sheen of ice on the outside of the window told her the frost had come in hard overnight. Her breathe steamed in the air as she hurried into her work clothes. The chill air on her flesh shocking her out of her self-pity. Descending the stairs as softly as possible so as not to stir the others before their time. An ill woken babe would put the whole household to disorder faster than thunder could sour the milk.

She unbanked the fire and lit the lamps to banish the darkness. A rapping at the kitchen door reminded her she needed the household purse. Calling out for him to wait she hastened to the parlour to retrieve it. Money in hand she swiftly returned to open the door for Crow the Dairyman.

As he entered the kitchen the first rays of the sun broke over the horizon and made his hair appear like a golden red halo. Mary-Agnes felt the breath catch in her throat and she nearly fainted. Was this him? Adam Crow was a familiar but distant figure. His occasional deliveries were the only times he came to their home from the farm he worked with his father. Her mind raced seeking fresh details. His hair was definitely red, and he fitted the general shape from her dream. She cursed herself anew for ruining the spell, she inhaled deeply and there was definitely a slight hint of milk in the air, but he was carrying pails of it. Was it that simple?

She blushed and stammered her way through the transaction and polite small talk about the coming festivities. He gave no signs of being sweet on her, and after the initial shock she was all at odds and couldn't work out her own mind. Her sister soon joined them, the child swaddled, and half woken but still peaceful. Adam Crow smiled sweetly and congratulated Abigail on such a bonny child and made his excuses and headed back out into the cold to complete his deliveries.

Mary-Agnes, Abigail and with the occasional assistance from Aunt Grace saw the preparations for the christening feast move forward. Outside the day slowly brightened but remained chill. Mary-Agnes was chided a few times by Aunt Grace. When she over stirred the cream or nearly forgot to add salt to the bread. "Art thou mazed? Have the fae stolen away with thy wits girl? Take better care." She apologised and did her best to carry out her tasks, but her mind was elsewhere. The day passed in a blur, the rite saw her nephew named Thomas and a cheerful gathering of family and friends rounded the day off.

The next day Aunt Grace was waved off on her return journey and Mary-Agnes was glad to have her room to herself again. She began to plan. She had to see Adam Crow again and pursue her dream. It was just not going to be easy. Until an idea struck her, in the parlour that night she laid out her thoughts.

"Abby, I was a wondering, thou'st tried thy hardest but my embroidery stitching is still a most shocking thing. I thought might it not be a useful thing if I were to learn some other less dainty skills? Mayhaps I could see if Mrs Crow at the dairy might be willing to tell me of her butter and cheese work." She had thought about being more circumspect and trying to hint at it but she knew Abby was too sharp and a simple approach was the best.

"I can see why that would appeal more. Needlework is a slow steady task and ye have always been a fidget. It sounds a fine thing to learn. And mayhap Young Adam will be able to show ye a hand at the milking too." Abigail barely looked up from her stitching but Mary-Agnes felt her ears burn as her sister's comment hit too close to home.

"Aye, mayhaps." Mary-Agnes squeaked out. "I'll take a jaunt over first thing, and take her something to soften the way, if that is alright?"

"Aye, take some of the hedgerow jam, we've plenty and the tartness is more to Mrs Crow's taste than the strawberry if I recall." Abigail nodded and continued her work. She sighed inwardly as she felt the tension loosen that had been keeping Mary-Agnes on edge since even before the Christening. The Crow lad was an odd one, but it was good for Mary-Agnes to get out and maybe she would do him good too.

The next day started with a slow grey winter dawn, Mary-Agnes wrapped her shawl tightly around her head as she headed out of town. The clouds overhead heavy with their winter burden. The wind was erratic but stinging when it came, she could taste in the air the snow that was to come later. The way to the Crow farm was well known and deeply rutted from the generations of carts ladened with barrels of butter, milk, and cream. She was grateful that the cold frost had hardened the mud enough so that she didn't sink into it, especially as she crossed the farmyard to the muted lowing of the cattle in the barn.

The door into the cottage opened as she neared it and a figure appeared in the shadowy doorway.

"Welcome child. Come. come in, come in. What can I do for thee?" Mrs Crow beckoned her in out of the cold. "Bless my soul, is it not Mary-Agnes? What brings ye all the way up here?"

"Morning Mrs Crow. Aye, tis a fair pace, but a dry day for all that its fresh, so it could be worse. I've brought ye some of Abby's Hedgerow jam. If ye've a taste for it." She fished the jar out of her basket and placed it on the table. Having followed Mrs Crow into the kitchen. She felt the heat sting her face as the chill was driven from it by the warmth of the fire.

"That's most kind of ye, that is. Sit a spell and I'll put some tea on and ye can give me the news from o'er that side of the river. Mr Crow is not much of talker and Adam means well but he is not good for the gossip. How was the christening?" Mrs Crow set her kettle to boil and gestured Mary-Agnes to sit. The gentle chatter and exchange of news of everyone's health filled the time it took to boil the water and steep the tea.

"Now, I can tell ye have some other thing on yer mind. Tell me true. What brought thee up this way?" She set her cup down and fixed Mary-Agnes with a firm but friendly gaze.

"Oh, Mrs Crow I've a favour to ask that I didn't want to bring out first, as it felt unseemly to march to thy door, a near stranger and not sure how to askit." Mary-Agnes words stumbled from her tongue and in the silence stared down at her cup. She cradled it in her hands and looked as if she was trying to read the leaves for herself.

"Those as don't ask don't get. My mother, God rest her, always said. Ye aren't a child now but a young woman, so speak thy mind and let me judge mysel' what I'll do." Mrs Crow nodded and Mary-Agnes felt her courage grow.

"I've a wish to learn more skill, Mrs Crow. My Abigail talks highly of thy cheese and butter and I wondered if I might be able to ask of ye to teach me a little. I can help with aught that thou needst, I'm a cleanly one and so can help about the place but don't ask me much of the mending as my stitches tend to get all of tangle." Mary-Agnes words spilled forth like a melt water dam breaking. Mrs Crow smiled and took one of Mary-Agnes' hands from the cup.

"Fret not child, it sounds a fair request and I'm sure there are tasks that will be made the lighter for having two pairs of hands. Adam and

Mr Crow are busy, even this season so good company and a willing helper is ne'er amiss. I make less in the winter, but can share with ye the basics, and if ye can make a simple cheese with winter milk thou'lt have less to learn come the summer." Mary-Agnes smiled in relief at Mrs Crow words.

"Oh! Thank ye Mrs Crow. That is most kind. I'll be such a learner as ye've not had before." She clasped the older woman's hands in hers in gratitude.

"Call me Rachel" Mrs Crow urged her and then set Mary-Agnes to making a fresh pot of tea while they discussed the plans. Come lunchtime when Adam and Mr Crow returned she was feeling almost at home.

"What's this? Another mouth for lunch? Why have ye tarried here lass?" Mr Crow queried when he saw the table set for four.

"Hush now Mr Crow, is naught but a bit of broth and bread. Mary-Agnes here is set to learn some dairy skills from me and lend her hand to tasks whilst ye are out tending the herd. Has been a harder time of late. Ye recall." Mrs Crow kept her voice even, but Mary-Agnes could see from the corner of her eye the careful stillness that had come over the woman. Having been so relaxed before she felt the air shift and copied Rachel's lead where she could. Making herself smaller by sheer effort of will.

"Pah, as ye say. As long as she is not a greedy one be sure to get thy worth of work from her, and she is not to be a burden to thy day. I expect to see more done, but the house is thine to run. Just see to it." The meal passed in deep quiet after that, other than news exchanged of the herd and the tasks that still awaited. Adam kept his head down but shyly nodded his thanks when Mary-Agnes passed the butter when she saw that he couldn't reach it. The room felt lighter when Mr Crow and Adam left again to return to their chores. Rachel Crow was a knowledgeable and kindly teacher and Mary-Agnes felt the shape of what she might learn from her over the coming weeks.

"That is enough for now child." Rachel declared. They had finished the lesson and been sharing some of the tasks ahead of the evening meal. "The sun doesn't have much longer and we don't want thee walking that road in the dusk if we can avoid it." Mary-Agnes nodded. She heard the unspoken reminder that she had better be gone before Mr Crow returns.

"Aye, I'll get my shawl and be on my way. Thank ye so much Rachel." The older woman smiled but looked weary, the thin light of the winter afternoon made the fine lines appearing by her eyes look more pronounced. "I'll be back the day after the morrow."

She bundled herself up and made for the road. The wind was just as biting as this morning, but Mary-Agnes walked with her head held higher. She was on the right path. She was sure of it. The trip home seemed to be over in a flash and soon was gushing to Abigail about the kindness of Rachel Crow and the plans that they had made to teach her the dairy skills she sought.

The easy pattern grew of alternate days with the Crows and time at home with Abigail, Jacob and little Thomas. Mr Crow remained dour and grudging of any hospitality. Adam remained polite but distant. Mary-Agnes tried on occasion to 'accidentally' brush her hand on his but when she succeeded he stammered an apology for his clumsiness and retreated. Her last visit had ended early as Mr Crow had returned home early and the fear that came to Rachel's face had quite unnerved Mary-Agnes and when pressed she had only said "He is a man of strict regular habits any variations bodes ill. At least it is not a late one." Before she had hushed her pupil and sent on her way.

At her next visit Mary-Agnes decided to see what she could learn about her other project. "Has Adam always been a shy one?" Mary-Agnes asked Rachel. Gentle chatter while operating the churn made the monotonous task that touch more social. Rachel had even been teaching her some songs, but today she had been more withdrawn.

"Adam? Aye. Well of late. He has grown more thoughtful this last year. The bullish youth has gone from him, but he is a steady lad now. And his heart is good. Last winter was hard on him." Mary-Agnes risked a glance up. Rachel's face had softened but she looked out the window rather than at her companion.

"Last Winter?" Mary-Agnes enquired. "Aye. Since Poor Iain passed, God rest him. They were close." A shadow of sadness passed over Rachel's face.

"He was a good friend?" Mary-Agnes asked trying to understand better the man she believed was fated for her.

"Aye. Few closer and better than the pair of them." Rachel's face became hard and her eyes remote. "Ye are getting sloppy with that churn girl. Pay better mind." Mary-Agnes felt the heat reach her face and stared hard at her hands getting a firmer grip on the paddle. They continued in silence for the rest of the lesson. When they got up to return to the kitchen Mary-Agnes saw Rachel stumble and she went to catch her arm. Rachel gasped at the touch and struggled away from Mary-Agnes' grasp.

"Are ye unwell? Ye look truly pale." Mary-Agnes asked Rachel. The older woman struggled to compose herself.

"Just a moment's silliness. Right as rain now." She refused to look at the young woman. "Let's get back to set the lunch. The men will be here soon. And I would say a wise word to thee girl. Mention not Iain to neither Adam nor Mr Crow. What's buried is best kept that way." She hurried out across the yard and Mary-Agnes trailed behind, having halted to secure the workroom door. The lunch was even more grim than normal. The food was still hearty and warm, but the chill that hung about the family took the savour from her mouth. The afternoon passed slowly, the ever-creeping darkness meant the afternoon lessons shortened and shortened. This time Mary-Agnes was grateful when Rachel decreed they were done for the day and she was free to go.

That evening when she joined Abigail and Jacob in the parlour after dinner, Mary-Agnes sighed heavily into a chair by a lamp. She pointedly ignored Abigail's raised eyebrow when she picked up a much-neglected mending project and settled herself to the task. The fire crackled cheerfully but the atmosphere was not lively, Mary-Agnes sighed again and tried to attend to her stitches.

"What ails ye woman? Ye've been a damp mop e'er since ye got in. And ye even came home early. Were ye a lax pupil? Did ye get a scolding?" Jacob enquired, his attention easily drawn from his correspondence.

"Nay. Nowt of that ilk. It was just that there was such a thundercloud over the Crows today. Rachel Crow was right out of sorts." Mary-Agnes looked over at her brother in law.

"Oh. Aye. I'm not surprised, that place is often under a Thundercloud, by name of Mr Crow. It shocks me that all of their milk isn't curdled when they pull it from the teats, he is such a sour one." Jacob cheerfully set to dissecting the personality of Mr Crow. "That Rachel Crow is either a saint or part angel as the whole parish wonders how she bears that man."

"But he was'ne even there. I just asked about Adam and why he was so sad over his friend Iain." Mary-Agnes interjected. A stiff silence fell over the parlour. Jacob open and closed his mouth a couple of times and his face coloured a little.

"Oh. That. Well. I think mayhaps it….." he began to stammer out and as the flow of words increased a sudden bang disrupted his flow. Abigail picked up her book from the floor and clutched it to her chest.

"I think that we had best not bring this up. I'll not have ye speaking ill of the dead in this house Jacob Stone and I know how they felt about Iain MacDonald, God rest his poor soul. So, none of this now. Mary-Agnes, I'll advise thee as a sister should, if ye were asking after that then I say hold thy tongue in future. It is a matter best left unbroached. I wonder not that Rachel Crow sent thee home early. Such a sticky beak I've not known. Ye were lucky to not have a flea in yer ear to go with the early dismissal." Abigail's voice was firm and even.

"Aye Abby. I hear thee and I'll not utter one word on't again. I'm feeling weary all of a sudden, I'll retire. Good night to ye both." Mary-Agnes fled the parlour, her needlework abandoned on the floor. Her eyes misting she threw herself on the bed and let the anguished sobs silently wrack her body. "It's not fair." She muttered to herself over and over until she fell asleep fully clothed.

The next few visits to the Crow far were formal but less frosty. Rachel greeted her more warmly each time and gradually returned to her gentle mode of instruction. As the winter deepened the lessons became more stories of what she needed to know and theory whilst they worked on small tasks. Preparing lunch one day the sky had darkened so much by noon that they lit the lamps to aid their work. The door opened abruptly, and Mr Crow entered.

"There is a snow front coming in." He said gruffly. "We will need to eat quickly and we have one final delivery to do before it breaks." Without exchanging a word Mary-Agnes and Rachel fell to preparing the lunch things. The broth had been already set to warm so a quick stoke of the fire got it back to a simmer. They ate quickly and mostly in silence.

"If the weather is to be bad, I suggest Mary-Agnes that thee head back to thy sister's home. It would be a rough night for all and not much comfort for us to bed ye here. And if the snow makes the road bad it might be a few days, which would never do, no not at all." Rachel suggested and Mary-Agnes nodded. Whilst she liked the idea of being near to Adam and seeing if she could wring more than two words from him. The idea of being under the same roof as an unhappy Mr Crow for longer than necessary was enough to have her reaching for her shawl with only a moment's pause.

"I'll take her." Adam said unexpectedly into the silence. "Da, thou needst to stay and secure the black heifer ye knowst she needs thy firm hand. Once ye've helped me load the cart I can take it and drop Mary-Agnes in the village on my way to the manor. I'll be back afore dark and whilst the snow's not too deep even if it were to start now." It was the most Mary-Agnes had ever heard him speak unprompted. Matter of fact and gentle, but not seeming anything other than practical. Her eyes darted back and forth between Adam and Mr Crow. Mr Crow slowly chewed his mouthful of bread.

"Aye. makes sense." He nodded and went back to his broth. Rachel Crow nodded at her son and gently squeezed Mary-Agnes hand fleetingly as she passed taking her bowl to the sink. Mr Crow stood and shouldered his way back into his overcoat. Adam followed him and Mary-Agnes set to helping Rachel set the kitchen to rights. They didn't speak until they heard the cart pulling up outside.

"I think that this'll be our last lesson until the days begin to lengthen again. The winter is set to worsen come the solstice and I'll not want ye freezing just to learn some dairy skills." Here take these." Rachel packed a few of the soft cheeses she had taught Mary-Agnes how to make and a small pat of butter from the batch she had churned. Mary-Agnes kissed Rachel lightly on the cheek.

"Thank ye kindly Rachel, ye art a right good teacher." she bobbed a little curtsey of thanks. Rachel smiled kindly in response. "Ye are a good woman. Mary-Agnes, and learning well. But I think ye need to find a man with the heart to love ye and don't just fall for a false dream." Mary-Agnes started at these words as they sounded more warning than blessing. She blushed as she felt Rachel had seen through her. She stammered thanks and was then bundled out of the house and onto the waiting cart. Adam didn't speak until they had cleared the gate.

"We will get thee home before it gets too bad. The cart will spare ye the worse of the ice. It is already treacherous." He kept his eyes fixed on the road and his hands in this rough gloves on the reins. Mary-Agnes muttered her thanks through her thick shawl but didn't know what else to say. She snuck sideways glances at him please that they were finally alone but didn't feel the fluttering in her heart that she had hoped would grow. A small lock of red hair stuck out from his knitted cap but in the darkening afternoon it looked more of a ruddy brown than the copper red of her dream. With that realisation and Rachel's warning she felt her heart sinking. It had all been for nought. She was not in love.

The cart trundled along the rutted road. The rattle of the wheels only accompanied by the sharpening howl of the wind. The horse as familiar with the route as the driver and needed little encouragement to keep moving, his ears flicking against the wind.

The last hill before the descent to the river came and the horse strained up it. A new jarring note joined the familiar rumble. An offbeat rattle. As the cart reached the peak and began the descent both Mary-Agnes and Adam found their attention being pulled behind them. Squinting against the bitter wind, she found the source, the smallest barrel on the top of the load was working itself loose as the cart jostled over the rutted road.

"Canst thou see what is amiss?" Adam asked his attention torn between the road and the worrying sound behind them.

"Aye." She began, "It is..." she was cut off by a scared whinny from the horse and the sensation that the cart was sliding sideways, alarmingly fast. Adam pulled tight on the reins and reached down for the brake, struggling to control the cart in its unexpected movement. Mary-Agnes heard a sudden cry of fear from behind her, but she echoed it with her own as she was partly thrown into the back of the cart by Adam's successful attempt to bring it to a stop. From her half prone position, she watched the small barrel that had been working itself loose teetering from its unsteady perch and bounce away. Striking the edge of the cart, the barrel split and a fountain of milk arose and disappeared over the side. There was a second half drowned cry from the roadside.

Adam's face appeared over her now that the cart had stopped moving. "Art thou well?" He asked his own face white from the recent strain, his lips compressed into a flat line.

"Aye, a bit tumbled, but nothing broken." Mary-Agnes replied. She hadn't realised her heart was pounding from the fall but as the danger passed she felt it slow and her breathing became more even.

"But I'm not! I'm a sodden mess! All over milk and ye damn near ran me over!" A much more unhappy voice piped up from the side of the cart. It was quickly joined by a very angry and very wet looking young man. As he arose and settled his dripping arms on the side of cart, there was an overwhelming smell of milk. Mary-Agnes found her heart beating faster again. The memory of her dream flooding her mind. The man reached up and took off his milk drenched cap, and began to wring it out. His hair underneath was bright red. As shiny as burnished copper. Mary-Agnes' breath caught in her throat.

"John? Is that ye Cuz?" Adam sounded shocked. Mary-Agnes looked backwards and forwards between the two men. Her heart skipped when she looked at John but nary a flutter with Adam.

"Adam? Aye. It is me, coming to visit thee all I was. Sent to bring a message from mother to Aunt Rachel, and Uncle Crow. And what happens but ye try and run me down and drown me both!" He began to laugh a deep rich sound that invited them to join him. Soon all three were near mad with laughter and tears standing in their eyes.

Adam pulled his cousin up into the cart and after covering him with a spare blanket from the back they set off again. The auburn-haired stranger sat between them smelling of milk. He was smiling and joking with them both as they carried on their errand, refusing any suggestion he go back alone as he would rather be huddled on a cart than walking sodden in the wind.

Mary-Agnes smiled at him and unwrapped her shawl to allow her to talk more easily with him even in the face of the rising winds. Mayhap dreams can come true, even if not always as ye expect them to.

The Secret Posey

The wind was whipping wildly through the muddy streets. The few traces of snow that hadn't become slush flurried back into the air. An unusual thaw had struck but the folks of the village all agreed that a deeper freeze was coming. It was in their bones, every twinge foretold another snowfall before long.

Constance Purkiss sat by the parlour window and watched the sky. Her thumbs had been pricking all day. Mother Beecham had nodded when she had mentioned it. "Is an ill wind. And more is afoot than ye knows yet. My rheumatiz tells me the weather and the sight tells me there is ill abroad. We'll see more afore the moon's full, mark it."

Constance had hoped she would explain what she meant, but whilst she was yet learning, Mother Beecham wasn't quite teaching. The summer and autumn had been full of growing and gathering and all of the practicalities of making a store of the essentials. Mother Beecham was slowing down, despite her best efforts to be immortal, which is why Constance had come to help her. Constance found snippets of lore had the habit of being given as throw away comments, but without the context that might have helped her make total sense of it. Everyday Constance feared Mother Beecham's wits were more scattered than the leaves blown from the trees. So, she bided her time, took notes and made herself useful with the mending and the making that was her joy and skill. The delicate flowers of her embroidery were taking shape in the lamplight that was their only bulwark against the gathering night. She moved her seat from the window to the low stool near Mother Beecham and the lamp.

"What shall we have for supper?" She asked her eyes focused on the delicate play of needle and thread in her steady hands.

"We'll be having a guest soon. Get the cold ends out and this morning's bread. And the nice pickle." Mother Beecham was sat staring at the darkening sky, her head nodding gently in time to a rhythm that Constance couldn't hear.

"A guest? Ye never said one was expected!" Constance looked up and scrutinised her erratic teacher, but she could see no sign that the older woman had even heard.

"Aye, nor was she. But still she comes, and bide she will, at least a short space. Heavy is her heart, and the sky is not the only thing darkening." Mother Beecham sucked on her few remaining teeth. The familiar noise unsettling Constance as it was a bad sign. She redoubled her efforts to finish the current embroidered bloom. It was a source of frustration when she had to stop midway through one.

The sudden rapping at the door made her start and she jabbed herself with the needle. Quickly pulling her hand away from the cloth to stop her blood staining the fabric. A single drop of blood welled on her finger and she quickly put it in her mouth and sucked.

"Get the door. She is awaiting and needs our counsel." Mother Beecham rearranged her skirts and settled herself to face into the room. Constance carefully laid her handiwork down and swiftly walked the few paces to the door. Opening it she found their visitor in the action of leaving, their body turning away. They abruptly stopped as they heard the door open. The face that turned towards her from the darkness was one Constance recognised immediately, although it was unusually pale and heavily tear-streaked.

"Susan Kane? Come in out the cold, whatever is amiss?" Constance stepped back and Susan quickly slipped through the door and closed it behind herself. Leaning against it, her green eyes darted around the room. She remained poised ready to flee at any moment.

"Mistress Purkiss, Mother Beecham. Begging yer pardon for this intrusion." She stuttered her greeting, not once did she let her eyes linger on any one spot for more than an instant.

"Come in, come in. Thou'st not doing any a favour by loitering at the threshold. Ye've crosst it now and may as well sit awhile." Mother Beecham beckoned her in. Nodding to Constance who went to help Susan out of her heavy shawl. Susan's hair normally so beautifully arranged was covered with a heavy plain kerchief, pinned tight to her head. Constance got a small shock like tiny lightning in the dim room when her hand brushed Susan's shoulder as she took the shawl. It went to ground in the pricking in her thumbs like a bird roosting in its nest. Mother Beecham saw the widening of Constance's eyes and quickly shook her head, nodding towards the hearth. Constance nodded in response. She would follow Mother Beecham's lead and went to stoke the fire and prepare their food.

Constance thought over what she knew of Susan. A local fieldworker at the Viscount's nearer farm. A robust girl, but a kindly one. She smiled less than she would for someone of such good spirits as she was conscious of her gap tooth. She was a handy girl and strong. She was also a social creature often found in the village sharing news, so she was a familiar face in the village, even to Constance who was a relative newcomer.

There had been several incomers from that summer who had lingered after the weather turned cooler. Constance was one of them and had been visiting Mother Beecham regularly for a year and more frequently over the months preceding her move. This meant that she was treated less as a stranger and more as a distant relative who had decided to bide. Her position in Mother Beecham's household had meant the villagers had accepted her immediately. It was only the priest that had been distinctly cold when he realised that 'Mother Beecham's help meet' as he called her was just as unimpressed by him as his more elderly parishioner. He had been more vocal in his praise of the other new member of his flock, his elderly housekeeper's niece who was lending a hand in his household. Mother Beecham had seen her at a distance and had taken to referring to her as 'that pious mouse' and had dismissed her from consideration.

Susan finally took the chair that Mother Beecham had offered her. The air was thick with the fear that was coming off the young woman. She kept her eyes fixed downwards, looking sideways into the shadowy corners of the room. Her ill ease so intense that Constance found her own eyes checking those same shadows until she caught herself in the contagion of fear and settled her own mind. Making a quick pot of tea ahead of the supper Constance watched Mother Beecham and Susan closely. The old woman approached the young girl as if as was calming a wild animal. Mother Beecham avoided sudden movements and she began talking in a gentle babble about the weather and the season and the goings on in the village. Susan slowly seemed to be melting out of her fright and when she was presented with the tea she gratefully held it in her hands. She sat on her chair and cautiously watched the other women. Once she saw them drink from their own cups she sniffed it suspiciously once but then sipped it carefully. The tears began to well in her eyes once more.

"Oh, Mother Beecham, forgive me! I'm right sorry, I am! I never meant to offend ye. Please, undo it. Take it back. I'll do what e'er ye ask. Just take off the curse!" Susan nearly dropped the cup of tea and Constance started to catch it as she dropped her head into her hands and began sobbing wildly. Both of the witches were equally shocked by this outburst, Constance was a little relieved that Mother Beecham was also taken aback. Susan threw herself on her knees in front of Mother Beecham and began to clutch at her skirts. Repeatedly begging for forgiveness.

The elderly witch rested her hand on the kerchief covering Susan's hair, the same spark of wild fire danced across her fingers. Mother Beecham's eyes went as hard as stone.

"Nay Child, it is not my doing that had brought this hex on ye. I feel it right strong, but I promise thee by fire and stone I have not raised my will against thee, no matter what thou mayst think called down my ire. Tell me more of it." Her eyes became kindly again when Susan collapsed back on her heels and looked up at the old witch.

"Truly? Thou ain't the one that hexed me?" Susan turned around and glared at Constance, the unspoken accusation clear.

"Susan, I promise thee too by Fire and Stone that I bear thee no ill will and have not raised my will agin thee." She raised her hands to her heart and let the girl see her honest compassion.

She nodded once and her face crumpled as the tears returned. Mother Beecham and Constance's eyes locked. The ill portents had focused on this young woman and she needed help.

"Hush, hush child. Speak thy part and we'll see what mayst be done." Mother Beecham offered the young woman a handkerchief from her sleeve to dry her eyes. The tears had made their green even more startling against her pale skin. Susan took a deep breath and reached up to remove the kerchief that she had anchored securely to her head. As it came free so did the hair. Both women were shocked as what before had been a dark mane, thick and silky that the young woman had been rightly proud of was now worse than a bird's nest. It was a riot of strange colours and textures which formed into a knotted tangle that seemed to have nothing but split ends. It swamped her head and seemed almost alive once it had been freed from confinement. Constance's mouth dropped open and her hand flew to cover it, her eyes widening at the sight. Mother Beecham's lips pursed a little but she was clearly fascinated by what she was seeing.

"The author of this curse was inventive and powerful. But we'll see thee right child. I feel a touch of cruelty in this too. She's a mean one, who'er she might be. This has the whiff of malice in it, bitter as sulphur." Mother Beecham waved her hands around the girl's head feeling the strands of the curse. "She must have a bit of thy hair to do this. We will need to undo it and give thee a ward agin her too. I'll set to the unravelling and Constance here will make thee up a charm to keep thee safe." Constance smiled tightly, her eyes gleaming with the pride of being entrusted with making the counter spell. She nodded quickly and turned towards the press where they kept the ingredients.

"After Supper!" Mother Beecham snapped and Constance blushed deeply and set about gathering the food that Mother Beecham had instructed earlier.

The light meal passed quickly and with little conversation. Constance had also been set to put some water to heat for Mother Beecham's part in the cure. By the time they had eaten the water in the copper kettle and pans were beginning to steam gently. Constance had observed small signs over dinner that Mother Beecham was preparing the girl in other ways as well. The fragments of conversation had been subtle ways to gather helpful news. Small hints of likely enmity which would be squirreled out, her habits of brushing her hair and where she kept her brush. She was seeking clues as to who the other witch might be or how they had gotten Susan's hair as a likely ingredient in the curse.

Constance cleared the plates and put them by the sink to stand whilst she did the more urgent task of making the charm. Mother Beecham waved her away from the store cabinet whilst she gathered the ingredients she needed for the first part of spell. Susan sat frozen in her chair her eyes widening as the mystical preparations unfolded in the kitchen. Her hand began to stray towards the tangled and distorted mess, but she couldn't bring herself to touch it. Constance smiled reassuringly at her whilst she carried the large copper kettle over to the kitchen table and placed a small earthenware jug by it and the good basin to catching the runoff water. She settled a small pile of drying rags by the side of the jug as well.

Mother Beecham surveyed the set up and nodded as she hobbled her way back from the cupboard. Constance's mouth tightened as she tried not to smile broadly at the implicit praise. Reaching the table the elder witch scattered some herbs into the water and muttered words that Constance strained to hear but she was unable to make them out.

She now had her own task to complete. She settled her mind as well as she was able to weave the magics that would prevent the poor woman being victim to another attack. Mother Beecham began a gentle and tuneless humming that for all its low volume penetrated the room and weaselled its way into Constance's mind until she realised and tuned it out. That aspect of the soothing magic was meant for Susan but the calming vibrations in the aether helped the younger witch connect to her own powers. Soon a gentle counterpoint echo was emanating from her as she worked.

Constance's knowledge of herbs was profound for both medicine and magics, so she started with betony, vervain, mugwort and mistletoe. Once she set them out she let her intuition guide her further. Under her hands the various flowers and leaves were sorted and a plan began to form. Taking those with longer stems and a piece of ribbon from her sewing box she began to weave them into a posey of dried plants. The smaller blooms or loose large leaves she sewed into the bundle, the thread dancing through it as she worked. Pulling together and powering the charm with the magics of her will and wakening the power of the plants. As her eyes adjusted to the working so she saw the threads of magic spread through the posey as it formed. At its heart she placed a fresh sprig of Mistletoe. As she went to begin the final binding Mother Beecham's hand stayed her own, Constance startled at the interruption. In her altered state she had not perceived Mother Beecham's approach.

"Sorry Constance, I meant not to startle thee, but think that thee might find this of use before ye seal the charm." Mother Beecham sounded calm, but the reediness that lately came to her voice when she tired was more pronounced than Constance had heard it before. In Mother Beecham's fingers was a single strand of Susan's hair. Long and beautiful. Constance saw that it was now free of any taint of the curse and would anchor the charm more tightly to Susan. It would aid her if she were ever temporarily parted from it as long as it was close by. Constance nodded and delicately took the proffered hair. Weaving the strand into the posey took but moment and then drawing tight the overall ribbon Constance sealed the charm to do its work. For a moment in her eyes it shimmered golden and the dried flowers once more looked fresh. The flash of magic passed but it felt a little warm in her hands, although now it looked like any other bundle of dried flowers. Beautiful, but not unusual.

"Fine working there Miss Constance Purkiss. Perhaps ye'll do after all." Mother

Beecham's praise, even with the implied criticism of her past performance was enough to bring a fresh smile to Constance's face. Looking around she saw Susan curled up dozing in one of the chairs by the fire. The young woman's hair drying fanned out around her once again smoothly lustrous and shining black. Whoever had cursed her had selected her target well, the girl's hair was a sight to envy. Constance's heart fluttered in sympathy as she surveyed the simple innocence that suffused Susan's sleeping face, it made her look much younger than her years, and they weren't that many to begin with.

"Thank ye kindly Mother Beecham. I'm right glad that it meets thy approval. And that is a much-improved state in which ye have left our young lady." Constance returned the compliment to her teacher. Mother Beecham nodded in return. They gently woke Susan and explained to them what she needed to do. The posey would protect her if she kept it close. She should wear it every day, preferably out of sight and not put it aside even when she slept. Susan's eyes brimmed with tears as she professed her thanks. As she departed later she kissed the hands of the two women, her previous fear dissolved by their kindness. Mother Beecham and Constance safely disposed of the cursed water at dawn the next day. They poured it into the midden with a few charms to release the remaining malign force that had left it murky and threatening.

The next day the wind blew from the north and the predicted chill returned with a bitter frost that hardened the ground. Constance and Mother Beecham went about offering aid where needed to those who had taken a chill or a tumble on the ice. Susan returned to their cottage a few days later all smiles and thanks. No charge was ever asked but she gave them preserves and some dried apples from her stores in gratitude.

Come the next Sunday the wind had died down again and the sky was a crystal blue. Susan's breath steamed in the air as she made her way to church. Passing the smithy, she smiled happily when Amos slipped out from his master's house and shyly squeezed her hand as they made their way together to the service. She wouldn't be able to sit with him once they arrived, so these stolen moments were all that they had until he was as good as his troth and married her in the spring.

Her free hand went to the green St Audrey ribbon that she wore around her throat, his gift to her in the autumn when he had returned from his master's errands down south. She smiled at the memory of his bashful words "No, as green as yer beautiful eyes but matches em pretty good." His own cornflower blue eyes set in the square and kindly face. She always felt tiny next to him, but safe, like a squirrel sheltering in the lee of an oak. As an apprentice blacksmith he was all bulky muscles and slow seriousness. In her dreams she yearned for the day when she would be able to be with him for longer than the time they had betwixt the smithy to the church each Sunday.

She stole a peck on his cheek at the churchyard gate and then hurried in ahead of him to sit with her fellows from the Viscount's farm in the pew that the family had established for their workers and required them to use.

Amos entered soon afterwards and went to sit with his master Abel Smith, the blacksmith and his wife. They merely nodded at his late arrival and settled him alongside them. They had taken him in as both apprentice and over the years had become their surrogate child, so they were unashamedly indulgent of him. The service commenced soon afterwards and passed in the normal dull haze of comforting ritual and formulaic words.

Once the service was over Susan hurried out so she could position herself to wait for the second stolen moment when Amos would normally walk her home. As she reached the door there was some commotion behind her in the aisle, looking back she was unable to see what was happening due to the press of people exiting into the cold morning. Standing in the lee of the church the wind blew less harshly but she could see her breath in the air as she exchanged pleasantries with her neighbours as they made their way to their homes. As the crowd thinned the last people to come from the church were the Smiths, but with no sign of Amos. Their kindly faces were creased into frowns of concern as they made their way over to speak to her.

"Now, come along with us Susan, we'll walk thee part the way and let thee know what befell just now." Mrs Smith tried to take Susan's elbow to guide her. Susan stood as firm as a stone, her eyes darting back to the church and then searching the faces of her elderly neighbours.

"What's amiss? Where is Amos?" She felt her voice crack despite the effort to keep it level. The Smiths exchanged a worried glance.

"She said not to say" Mrs Smith began her eyes searching Susan's face, her husband's and on occasion the sky as if seeking inspiration.

"Hush now, that busy body would have all lips silent other than hers at command or none but when speaking other's secrets. The poor girl needs to know to ease her worry." Mr Smith patted his wife's hand and went to take Susan's elbow before he continued.

"Now as thee knows Mistress Fairley has been unwell of late and her niece Ruth has been helping out as a good soul should. But it seems the exertions have been a bit much for the poor girl and she took a turn at the end of the service and fainted dead away. If our young Amos hadn't been there she might have done herself a mischief, but he caught her in her swoon. Her aunt made it clear that Amos should carry her back to their house and that none of us were to speak a word." As the words flowed Susan relaxed and began to walk with the Smiths. Amos was doing a good deed and she smothered the envy that Ruth Fairley was even now being cradled in the arms that she had been dreaming about. She felt that they were hers by right of his promise but she could allow this kindness. The Smiths idle chatter as they walked through the village washed over Susan and she made little comment. The absence of her betrothed made the winter feel colder and the lonely walk back to the worker's cottage felt longer.

The next day Susan volunteered to collect the empty sacks from the village store. It was a cold walk but it was her way to get back into the village to speak to Amos. She rejected all offers of help from the others on the farm, easily done as they were half hearted at best with the other chores that would keep them warmer. A lot of things were preferred to a cold walk and a dirty load of bundled sacks. For Susan they represented freedom and a chance for some happiness.

As she neared the village she could see the smoke from the smithy rising straight against the pale clear sky. Although the day was still the ground felt as if it were sucking the heat from her bones with every step, so her teeth were chattering before she was halfway to the village. Making a beeline to the smithy she hurried into the darkness through the open door, the sudden change took her breath away and her made face sting as if she had been slapped. Brought short by the sensation and needing to adjust to the darkness she paused just after the threshold. As her sight adjusted she saw Mr Smith was absorbed in a corner over his order books in the glow of a lamp and Amos was looking deep into the fire in the furnace and holding a pair of bellows.

"Good Morrow both!" She called cheerfully once her voice returned, her heart warmed at the sight of Amos. Mr Smith was startled at the interruption but once he recognised Susan he and nodded once and made a quick excuse and disappeared through the door into the house. Amos just stood there, his eyes flat and serious as they met her curious gaze, she faltered. "What is amiss Amos? Art thou unwell?" Susan finally closed the space between them, as she approached he crossed his arms. His blue eyes hostile and lacking their normal spark of merriment.

"Why art ye here? Tisn't the place for thee." His voice rough and unwelcoming. Susan stood before this monolith of a man whose powerful build now seemed as unyielding as the iron he reshaped. His words made her feel as if she had been slapped again. Nothing was making any sense she reached towards him but she faltered and let her hand fall.

"Amos? What can ye mean? I wanted to see ye, we never got our walk home. After ye had been so kind as to aid the Fairley girl, when she was taken poorly. She mayhaps had been starving herself as her aunt's cooking is right heavy I hear. Come Amos. Why are ye being so cold to me?"

Susan's eyes searched his face looking for any sign of the shy lover who she had been wooed by and won by over the past months. This man was a stranger to her, a hard heart replaced the one she had grown to love.

"Miss Fairley is a fine woman, not a girl. Right refined. And ye'll not spread idle gossip about her. Know thy place farm girl!" His face reddened and he hands came to his side as fists. Susan stepped away feeling his anger radiating from him hotter than the furnace.

"I thought my place was with ye. We were to be wed come spring. I love's ye Amos Wynne. What has happened?" Susan went to rest her cold hand on his arm, to see if touch could reach him where her words were failing. Tears stood in her eyes, Amos simply made a sound of disgust and she let her hand fall.

"I love thee not Susan. It was but a passing fancy, that is now dead. Ruth is the woman for me, and I'll ask thee to leave me be." Amos turned his back on her and commenced using the bellows to stoke the flames in the furnace. Susan stood silent watching her now no longer betrothed resolutely ignored her and carried on his work. The tears now flowed freely and sobbing loudly she fled out into the cold morning.

Constance looked up from her careful stirring of a decoction in the saucepan, the banging on the door was frantic. Mother Beecham started in her chair by the fire.

"Just resting me eyes. Who'sit?" She asked quickly resettling herself comfortably and smoothing her dress.

"It's Susan. Somm'at has happened. Thou saidst that who'ever it was wouldn't let it lie once we undid her spell. It seems that our mystery witch has made her next move." Constance accepted the knowledge as it came to her. The words flowing from her without her knowing. Taking the pan from the heat she hurried over to open the door and stepped quickly aside to allow Susan to tumble into the room. The woman fell to her knees and struggled to breath. Constance could see the tears still wet on her cheeks. Fetching a cup she filled it with water and handed Susan a handkerchief as she helped her to the chair by Mother Beecham. The elderly witch was scrutinising Susan carefully.

"Aye, ye're right. Though it is Amos this time and not Susan who has been bewitched." Mother Beecham nodded to Constance who gave a small half bow in response and she took Susan's hand. Settling her mind she exuded calm at the girl to help slow her breathing and to give her a chance to tell her tale. After a couple of sips of water she composed herself enough to speak. Her response was hesitant and her voice broke at points, but it was as they had divined. Susan's tale of Amos' betrayal was short but to the point. The name of his new beloved was met with disbelief by both Witches.

"Ruth Fairley? That little mouse? She is as limp as an ancient cabbage leaf. The few times she has dared to even be seen in the village she was naught but a pious greyling. I saw her simpering at the heels of that meddlesome priest. If she is a witch she has not a shred of pride in her to be so subservient to a man such as he. Pah. I say, there must be another at work." Mother Beecham's scorn flowed freely, Constance could feel the slight off-note jangle in the elder's tone, it was the echo of self-recrimination that they had both missed the signs if this was the case. She herself was wondering how she had missed it, shaking her head she focused back on the problem at hand.

"Mother Beecham, hush now. Whoever it is, our young smith is now under the thrall of a love spell and that ain't right. I think we need to act right quick too. It sounds like a cruel one if it made him so harsh so quick." Constance patted Susan's shoulder.

"Pah! Men don't need much encouragement to turn cruel, but normally tis after they got what they wanted." Mother Beecham riposted, the shocked look on the younger women's faces made her pause. "Tis the truth, but that is an old tale and not one that is being told here no doubt. Least said soonest mended." She raised herself out of the chair and went over to their store beckoning Constance to join her. They formed a plan in whispered conversation as Susan sat by in mute despair sipping her water. A short while later the door closed firmly behind the three women as they went on their mission. Constance using both hands to carry their fully ladened basket towards the village smithy.

Mother Beecham was panting a little from their haste when they reached the door to the smithy. It was now only slightly ajar and the air at the threshold wavered with the haze of the inner heat. Constance peeked around the door to see how things lay. In the dim interior she could see Mr Smith and Amos working the forge together. Reporting this to the others they all headed to the main door of the house which Mrs Smith quickly opened after their gentle knock.

"Now this is a lovely surprise. What can I do for ye all?" The joy in her voice drained away as she took in the tear-streaked face of Susan, Constance's serious eyes and the determined line of Mother Beecham's jaw.

"We thank ye for yer welcome Mrs Smith but there is trouble a foot, and a curse at work on thy young apprentice." Mother Beecham minced no words and the colour drained from Mrs Smith's face. "He is bewitched and has spurned young Susan here. No, don't speak." Mother Beecham held up her hand as Mrs Smith opened her mouth to object. "This is the second hex that we have been asked to deal with in this case. There is no doubt in my mind that there is a foul work at play and not just the fickle heart of a youth. I'll be having none of it in my village, and ye'll be wise to have none of it under thy own roof too." Mrs Smith nodded simply looking helplessly between the three women in her hallway.

"Now Mrs Smith, why don't thee take Susan to the kitchen and get the kettle on? Mother Beecham and I will go to the smithy and send Mr Smith through to thee for a cuppa. Whilst we have a word with young Amos and see what we can do to undo all this nonsense." Constance kindly patted Susan on the shoulder and watched as Mrs Smith wordlessly led the young woman into the kitchen.

"To work!" Mother Beecham declared as she opened the door from the house into the smithy. The sudden wave of heat misted their eyes for a moment, but soon they adjusted to the dim red light of the furnace. Mr Smith was just setting down his hammer and closely observing the horseshoe glowing in the big metal pincers. Amos was tending the fire so neither man noticed their entrance. Constance quickly marked the threshold that they had crossed with the salt that she had in her basket and quietly slipped through the shadows to do the same at the edges of the main door.

"Mr Smith!" Mother Beecham called out just after he had plunged the horseshoe he was working into the pail. The sudden cloud of steam surrounded her like a fiery aura and both men swore at what seemed like a devilish materialisation. "There is trouble in thy house. Good hearts are bent agin their own desires. I will have none of that darkness in my village. I bid thee head through to thy wife and I will heal thy troubled apprentice."

Mr Smith quickly regained his voice. "I hear thee Mother Beecham and right respected thee are in this village, but this is my house and I ken not what the trouble is of which ye are speaking. Amos is a fine lad and mayhap he has changed his heart but I ken not what issue it is of thine how the young may take their sport. I say thee are meddling where thou aren't needed." Mr Smith stood his ground and went to rest his hand on Amos' shoulder.

"Mr Smith! I say to thee that there is evil afoot. Will ye cross me in this?" Mother Beecham's voice rising in pitch as she encountered this unexpected resistance.

"Aye. I will. Unless Amos here wishes to speak with thee privately I'll none of this in my smithy." He resolutely crossed his arms and glared back.

"Amos. What is thy will? Will'st thou speak with us privately? I urge thee to hear Mother Beecham's warning and receive her aid" Constance's appearance from the other side of the smithy startled the two men again. Seeing their number evenly matched Mr Smith seemed to shrink back a little, as he was unable to keep a firm gaze on both Mother Beecham and Constance.

Amos seemed equally cowed by the situation and reluctantly nodded.

"I'll hear her out, but I promise nowt more. I said my piece to Susan and knowst my heart. Ruth is the woman for me, I'll none of that simpering farm girl henceforth." Amos crossed his arms and lowered his head, the picture of petulance.

"There now Mr Smith. Thou heardst him true. Amos will speak with us a while. Pray give us the grace of thy smithy. I think thy good wife willt have made the tea by now." Constance poured honeyed words to counter the bitter vinegar of Mother Beecham's anger. Mr Smith nodded and crossed into the house, his retreat less than graceful as he felt defeated in his own home, but as good as his word he shut the door behind him.

"Now Amos. I say that ye are bewitched. I ken that thee feels it not, but thy mind is entangled in another's snare. It makes thee wroth with that which ye love and love that which ye wouldst normally abhor." Mother Beecham now matched Constance's more gentle words. The two witches approached him slowly from either side. The muscular man's posture now shifting between petulant boy and cornered wild animal. They both began to hum softly to take the edges off his fear, and through the space that they had created in the smithy they began to weave their own snare for the huntress. Using her own prey against her.

"Amos, please come here and place thy hands on the anvil." Constance was closest and gently led the now more compliant man to the centre of the trap they were making. As he complied she then scattered a line of dried rowan berries around him in a horseshoe shape, the open-end pointed towards the outside door. Constance and Mother Beecham then took hands and stood just behind the apprentice smith. Their awareness of the spell binding him taking shape to their eyes like a dancing skein of light. Through his hand on the anvil they anchored one end of the spell into the iron and began to delicately pull on the remaining threads.

Their aim was to partially unravel the curse from his mind, but with each twist between them pulling tighter on the other end. The caster of the spell. By this chain of magic she would be summoned by her own working. The heat in the smithy made the air thick, and soon all three were sweating either at the effort of the spell weaving or the discomfort of its untangling. The minutes ticked by and the tension increased with each second. Like a fishing line with a hooked trout the

91

long thread of magic was dancing and resisting more as it tightened.

The door to the smithy flung open. The sudden burst of cold winter sunshine temporarily blinding them all. The lone figure struggled in, the compulsion of the magic that was their own doing pulling them along.

"Mistress Fairley?" Mother Beecham gasped as her eyes adjusted to the brighter light. "How canst be thee? I knew it was not that weakling girl, but still I would doubt my own eyes were thee not standing her so bound. Thou art naught but a pious old spinster not a witch! Hast thou grown bitter after all these years of housekeeping for the priest and hast it now turned thee to our path? Didst thou call the moon?"

Mistress Fairley spat at them. Her face distorted with the pain of the compulsion.

"I knew thou were an evil crone. Mother Beecham. What hast thou done to me? Why have I been brought here against my will? What are thou doing to young Amos? Release him at once? Release me too I say! I give not a farthing for your accusations. I am innocent and demand I be set free!" Mother Beecham began to pull at the final threads that bound Amos' mind.

"Me?! It is thou that hast bewitched this man to suit thy own ends. That mousey niece of thine hadn't the spirit to get herself her own man so thou stole one from poor Susan. Thou art the evil one here. Hiding behind thy pious mask, thou walk a darker path than I!" Mother Beecham almost spat at the bitterness in her words.

"Hold!" Constance shouted cutting across the squabbling of the older women. "Look Mother Beecham. Look at her shoulder!" Constance's eyes had remained tuned to the dancing skein of magic and saw a hint of something else. Almost invisible there was another string that led outwards from the smithy. A stray thread like those she controlled to embroider her flowers. She dug deep into the power and looped a part of the tangled magic around Mistress Fairley to hold her fast. This made it so she could reach this new unsuspected thread. Tugging the old woman into the heart of the trap as well and using part of the reversed flow of her curse she forced Mistress Fairley to also place her hand upon the anvil. This exertion brought fresh sweat to her brow as she compelled this reluctant obedience. Between them the two witches grounded this part of the curse back into the anvil and looked anew at what Constance had seen.

"Oh, that is a wily one!" Mother Beecham crowed as she too saw the slither of the additional magic that lead off from Mistress Fairley out into the world. Redoubling their efforts, the two witches pulled harder on this new strand. Whereas the love spell which had forced Amos to love Ruth was woven by Mistress Fairley they could now see that she was nothing but a puppet to another. There was a darker witch abroad who had bent Mistress Fairley to her will before using her to bind Amos. The sweat pouring off Constance stung her eyes, but she was not going to let this bigger fish escape.

This thread was more lively. The witch knew she had been caught, and was trying to play out the magic to break free. Mother Beecham leant against Constance whispering, "Take some more child." The surge of magic from the elder flowed down the connection strengthening Constance and a scream of outrage sounded outside the smithy door.

The scene before them was framed by the open doors and under the cold winter sun. Ruth Fairley was walking like a marionette towards the smithy. The power of her own curse now binding her own will to those who held the strings she had spun. Magic that comes from the blood and bone can be used against the caster, especially if they bind themselves as the master of another person. Controlling another's will or heart is the deepest and darkest use of magics, so it left Ruth powerless to resist the pull it exerted on her. She stumbled into the building the bright sunlight casting her in stark relief to the witches working in the fiery darkness of the smithy.

"We have ye now!" Constance shouted at her opponent. Reaching into her basket she pulled out a combination of dried flowers and herbs bound together into a wand. The fresh mistletoe still scattering berries as she waved it between Ruth and her victims. The final part of the spell was to shear through the last strands of the spell using the power of the plants and the intention of the witch wielding them. The broken threads of magic skittered around and earthed themselves in various parts of the smithy and the anvil in particular. Amos and Mistress Fairley both slumped to the ground. The abrupt severing of the mind control causing a whiplash effect that made them stumble at its abrupt absence. Mother Beecham looked pale but she bent to check them over whilst Constance faced down Ruth.

"So, that was right cunning. Using thy aunt as proxy like that to snare Amos. Thou art a cruel one Ruth Fairley. Why didst thou do it?" Constance walked closer to Ruth but kept her distance as even now she respected the other witch's power and malice.

"Susan is a gap-toothed simpleton. She don't deserve a proper man like Amos. And I'm not going to become a priest's slave like my aunt." She spat the last word. "Thou hast to take what thou want in this world. None will give it thee on a platter. Aunt Fairley wanted me to become like her. I needed an escape and when I couldn't make Amos not love her by ruining her one good feature I took him."

"Thou know that isn't the right way. Magic has a price and stealing people's minds is the darkest deed that any can do. Willst thou swear by stone and by fire that thou willst not try this again?" Constance stood before Ruth commanding her to make the oath. The wand still in her hand ready to block any new spell.

Ruth began to cry. "I'm just not able to get my luck am I?" Her face crumpled and she looked bleak. Ruth bent her head, her lank hair falling as a curtain over her face. She fell to the ground her hands moving frantically over the stone floor. Constance began to kneel down to comfort her. "Oh Ruth, we can show thee a better way. Weep not, thou just went a bit astray." Constance began but suddenly she felt herself overbalanced from behind as a figure barrelled into her snatching the wand from her hand.

Constance looked up to see Mother Beecham standing over her, holding up the wand. Her mouth dropped open in shock that she had been so assaulted. She turned back to see that Ruth was no longer cowering she had fallen to her knees. Her face was not heart broken, but was distorted with anger. The false repentance gone. Her hands began to rise like claws before her and were now snatching hungrily at the strands of her shredded magic. Reweaving it for her will. Constance then saw that her fall to her knees had been but a feint to gather some of the scattered salt and rowan berries for her own protection.

"Die! All of thee! None shall stand against me!" Ruth's hands beckoned and the fire from the furnace responded and began to dance through the air and send tendrils to lash each of the people in the smithy. Constance, Amos and Mistress Fairley covered against the onslaught. Through the roaring fire Constance heard Mother Beecham's angry response.

"Oh! Not in my village. I bind thee. By fire and stone, by blood and by bone. By these herbs I bind thy power to thy own skin. Not one breath beyond shall it extend." Mother Beecham dived forwards and grabbed one of Ruth's outstretched hands. With her other hand she slammed the wand into Ruth's forearm. The plants became incandescent, brighter than the furnace flame. Through the blinding flash of light they heard Ruth scream. The fire tendrils died from the air and an eerie silence fell over the room.

As her sense returned Constance looked at the other figures in the smithy. The inner door cracked open where Mr & Mrs Smith and Susan tentatively poked their heads around the door. Constance waved them in.

"Come help. See to Amos, and Mistress Fairley." her voice was now a croak. Next to her sat Mother Beecham breathing heavily with her eyes closed. After a gentle touch on the arm from Constance she opened them, but they looked glassy and distant even in the light from the outside.

"Tis done. But that took a lot." Mother Beecham closed her eyes again. Constance stood and walked the few paces to where Ruth Fairley had fallen unconscious on the ground. On her outstretched arm was a clear pattern of the wand, each of the different herbs clearly shown as a line drawing. The spell from Mother Beecham having now sealed her magic into her flesh.

"Come Mother Beecham. I think ye deserves a good cup of tea." Constance helped her elderly teacher up from the ground.

"That I do." Mother Beecham struggled to her feet and gently dusted off her skirts.

"What do we do with her?" Constance asked indicating the unconscious, and until recently, murderous witch.

"She is bound. Not a spell will work for her from this day until she dies. No witch will unbind her as they will feel the truth of her evil on her skin if she dares asks it of them. She will sleep for a while yet and her aunt will have the care of her once she wakes. But I feel Ruth Fairley will not bide here long. She can take her bitterness away, and not poison this place." Mother Beecham lent heavily on Constance's arm as they left the smithy.

"Aye. I think ye are right on that. Good riddance." Constance shut the door behind them and went to help their now defeated enemy's other victims.

The Mother's Prayer

"That all feels fine, Susan. Thou art doing well. Another few weeks and we will be seeing the little one. Are ye right sure thee don't want me to tell thee what the babe will be?" Constance Purkiss settled back on her heels and Susan Wynne shook her head firmly and began to tug her dress back down over her swollen belly. And settled her hand on it where she could feel the babe was growing restless in there. Her warm but weary smile showed off her gap teeth but was beautiful as it was lit from within by the glow of the love she was feeling for her child. Constance smiled back at her, happy that her duties of midwife were looking to be simple as all signs pointed towards it being a bonny babe born to a healthy and competent mother.

"Twill be a big un. And give the other two someone to boss around. Jamie is right keen to no longer be the littlest. If he had his way I'd have given them a younger brother or sister ages ago. Noah wants us to get a puppy and not another child, but that is the eldest for thee, not wanting to have to share further. Amos just smiles at them and me, so broad I think his head might fall off one of these days. Since Mr Smith retired after Mrs Smith passed, god rest her soul, Amos has been working even harder and saying less. But he smiles more. He loves that forge, so he does, so that is something." Susan finished rearranging her clothes for going back outside into the sharpening winds of early winter. The cutting chill made it necessary for her to swaddle herself in many layers. Her middle with the babe always felt warm, but her face took a chill so easily and so a headscarf and shawl crowned off her efforts. Bidding Constance farewell she went to complete her errands and relieve her friend who was minding her boys.

"Lottie! I'm back!" Susan called as she pushed open the door to the smithy cottage. Her feet and back aching, the basket feeling like it was filled with rocks rather than the simple shopping that she had gathered on her return from visiting Mistress Purkiss.

"Ah, there ye be. Let me take that." Lottie appeared from the kitchen wiping her hands on her apron and deftly taking the basket from Susan's unresisting hands so her friend could unwrap herself. "The boys are playing in their room. They've been as good as gold. All well with thee?" Lottie asked as they entered the kitchen and began unpacking the basket while Susan settled herself into a chair and made appreciative noises for being off her feet.

"Thank ye kindly Lottie. It is all good news from Mistress Purkiss. The babe will be with us before Yule if we've counted aright and all signs of health and vigour. I'm bruised from all her turnings and stretchings" Susan rubbed her side

101

where a vigorous punch or kick had just been made.

"She? Did Mistress Purkiss tell ye that?" Lottie asked as she went to put the kettle on. The deeply chilly breeze that had entered with her friend made her realise that a cup of tea was likely needed.

"Nay, she offered and all, but I just have a feeling that this will be a daughter after the other two. She just feels different. And so I am calling her a she. Although thee are the first I've told my thoughts. Foolish they may yet prove but I know what I feel and so I hold the dream a little longer." Lottie smiled at Susan, a tear forming in her eye as she settled down to pour the tea for them both.

"I've a secret for thee too. I've only just let on to Bill, but I am also expecting if I have counted the days right." Lottie's smile was nervous. Susan reached over and grabbed her friend's hand an excited smile brightening up her face.

"Oh, Mrs Charlotte Bass, that is perfect! Ye've not let on, such news. Let me see ye, not showing so it is right early still I'll wager. Now ye say and I look at thee proper there is a hint of the glow to thy cheeks, and here was me thinking it is just the winter chill adding to her rosiness. Are ye feeling well?" Susan appraised her friend and felt her initial excitement fade as she recalled that this was not the first time Lottie had been with child. The sad tale of such losses was not uncommon, but still put a finger of ice into her heart. She had also lost one of her babes before their time, so she knew the pain that came with that. And the fear. Even this time she had been as nervous as a maiden on her wedding night until the babe had given sign of quickening and she felt the life there.

"Aye, the normal, a touch of the morning sickness, but not too bad. All being well, will be with us before midsummer. It will be nice our bairns can play together when they are older." Lottie placed her hand on her belly, the ever so slight thickening she had discovered was hidden by her winter clothes. Susan reached out and placed her hand on top of her friend's.

"Aye. That is how it will be, best of friends. Now while the boys are busy, can ye take me over the plans for the hives again? Mrs Smith thought showing me once was enough to make me a beekeeper and since she passed, god rest her soul, I've not been able to keep on top of all the tasks and plans. Ye've been a god send to me, ye have indeed. Since we have the winter I want to go o'er it all." Lottie smiled and sat back down at the kitchen table.

"Of course. Let's start with the checks that ye'll need to do, I'll help!" Lottie's enthusiasm was contagious, and Susan felt her reluctance towards the tasks of beekeeping lessen. The presumption that she would carry on Mrs Smith's side-line of honey from the Smithy had been widespread. Any hint of reluctance was met with "But Mrs Wynne, it is a fine thing to do and such good honey. Ye'll not want to end a tradition." For a quiet life Susan had nodded, smiled and did her best for the hives. Lottie's help was making all the difference.

***

Charlotte began to clear the table. Bill had retreated to his workshop to put the final touches to a commission that the Viscount was going to want to collect tomorrow. The ornate leather shoes and matching belt were some of Bill's finest work to date. She smiled with pride that he was getting more recognition for his skill. There was a sudden pain in her side. The smile froze on her face. She dared not move. Then it came again, the plates in her hand fell to the table in a clatter.

She clutched her belly. The pain came again, the third time. A fiery poker running her through.

"No, No. No." she began uttering over and over again, the tears standing from her eyes. The pain came again in a rising wave of heat that tore through her middle. She felt a dampness start on her legs. She cried out as the next wave of pain brought her to her knees. She heard the door to the workshop open. Soft footsteps hurried closer.

"Fetch help. It's the babe. Something is wrong." She cried from the ground. The waves of pain increasing. She heard Bill hurry from the room and the distant banging of the front door. The moments blending together into a haze of pain and fear. She clutched her belly praying it would stop. It was an eternity of minutes later, filled with a constant roiling tide of pain, that she became aware of movement in the room and gentle but strong hands on her shoulders.

"Tell me, what ails ye." The voice was low and familiar. Charlotte looked up into the concerned and kindly face of Constance Purkiss.

"It's my, it's my baby. I am less than a couple of months along, but the pain..." She was interrupted again by a new wave of fire that tore through her body and left her shivering.

"Let's get thee off this floor. Give me a hand Mr Bass! Now Charlotte we'll get ye into thy bed and I'll see what we can do to set things right." Constance said her voice switching between firm and reassuring when addressing her patient. "Now Mr Bass if ye don't mind!" He opened his mouth, but the sight of his wife's pale frightened face and Constance's stern look kept him silent. He gently helped his wife upstairs with the midwife and left them to their examination.

Constance washed her hands in the basin on the sideboard. The water turning a woeful red. She looked over at the still pale but now sleeping face of Charlotte. The last hour had been difficult taxing Constance's skills and dangerous for Charlotte. It was fortunate that she was otherwise healthy and the blood loss was stopped or Mr Bass would have been a widower. The contents of the rag bundle she had placed in the other bowl had been without hope even before tonight. A cruel trick of nature that had made the woman think she was with child but all that was there was a mess of blood and nowt more.

Charlotte stirred when Constance went to take the bundle out of the room. Her pale eyes at first bleary but rapidly taking on a crystal-clear look of fear.

"My child?" She barely croaked the question. One hand tentatively going to her belly, her eyes searching Constance's face, the other reaching out. The simple shake of the head was all Constance needed to give, as the pain in her eyes added the rest. Charlotte began to cry. Constance slipped the bowl containing the rag bundle outside the bedroom door and returned to her patient's bedside.

"I'm sorry. I tried, but there was no child to save this time." She kept her voice low and warm, trying to comfort the grieving woman. She jumped back when Charlotte snarled at her.

"Thou art lying! Witch! Get away from me. I don't trust thee, it can't have been. Not again. This time it felt…" The angry words faded into sobbing. Constance shook her head and retreated, knowing that any attempt by her to comfort this woman now was going to fall on deaf ears.

"Mr Bass? Thy wife needs thee now. Comfort her, but best thou just be with her 'til the tears pass." Constance said to the worried man that she met on the stairs. His face went pale as his eyes darted to the red rag bundle in the basin. "I'm sorry for thee too. I'll take this away. It was not a child, I assure thee. Just a canker from the womb. She lost a deal of blood and must rest, tea and bone broth for a few days to strengthen her. But right now she needs thee and thou probably need her too." Constance let him pass and took the bundle of sorrow out of the house into the winter's night.

***

"Here Lottie. Hold Becky for me." Susan passed her daughter into Charlotte's hands. The winter was still biting deep outside so the plentiful layers of swaddling near swamped the babe.

"She is a bonny girl." Charlotte crooned as she opened the wrappings to have a better look at her friend's newest arrival. "Aren't thee now? And strong too!" Charlotte gasped when a pudgy fist sprang free from the loosened swaddling and grabbed her finger. The child pulling the finger closer to her mouth seeking to suckle.

"Oh, that she is. And a hungry mite too. I'm ready for her." Susan had been adjusting her shawl and dress to free her breast so she could feed her daughter. The tiny, but strong, fingers released their grasp when she sensed her mother was close and food was to hand.

"How are ye faring?" Susan's tone turned

solicitous. Now that her daughter was occupied she was able to turn her attention back to her friend. The small talk of the first part of their meeting done. Now it was time for the truth. The mother's eyes roved over her friend's face seeking signs of what was in her heart.

"I still ache. I feel so empty. Yule came and went, and not a spark of joy. I've kept apart from Bill too. The ache is worse when he is near. I hate that Witch Purkiss. I am sure she cursed the child." Charlotte's words sounded hollow.

"Hush now. I grieve that ye are still so heartsick, but I know Constance of old and not a bad bone is there in her. The ache is part of the loss. And as for Bill. Well, he will wait. Do what ye must. Ye knows that it is not a simple thing. Fate plays cruel tricks on us. Women with big hearts long to be holding a bairn of their own but are denied, and callow girls who took a quick tumble in the woods of a summer find their wild oats have taken root and flower unbidden. Tis not the first ye have lost, but I pray it will be the last."

Susan kept her eyes steady on her friend but could see no sign of the hoped-for thaw. The ice had gone deep and the wound too raw for kind reason to heal her.

"Thank ye Susan, but words cannae return what I lost, and I'm nay strong enough to bear more of this loss. It has quite hollowed me out." Charlotte's eyes stayed flat and listless, their depths concealing the tears she couldn't shed for fear of never ceasing.

"Lottie, I hope that come the spring ye'll see more light." Susan rocked her babe but her eyes stayed fixed on the still figure next to her. She could feel that the chill went to her friend's core and would take more than the change of the seasons to alter.

***

"Here ye go." Charlotte laid the fresh cool compress on Susan's forehead; her fever hadn't yet broken and it was proving to be a difficult winter.

Last spring's thaw came and went, and the seasons had rolled back to winter. The snows after Yule had brought with them a new illness. The Wynne household was just one of the many to be laid low with the raging fever. Charlotte had been lucky with her bout and it had passed off of after a few days of rest and some good care. Susan had seen her through and now it was Lottie's turn to help her friend. She had sent Bill off to visit his cousin so she could give her care and lighten the load from their busy household.

"Thank ye Lottie." Susan murmured. Her weakness had been worsening by the hour. Amos had retreated to the forge with the boys to try and keep them well. Setting up pallets there to make beds and treating it like an adventure, they were still scared but tried not to show it.

Rebecca had refused to go with them crying constantly when her mother was out of sight. For everyone's peace she was allowed to sit in the corner of the bedroom playing with her rag dog. Charlotte kept her away from Susan as much as possible, but always in line of sight until bedtime.

"I'll fetch ye some broth in a bit, see if that will set ye right." Charlotte maintained as cheerful a tone as she could.

The rash that had come with the fever was still angry looking on Susan's pale skin, the green of her eyes standing out more against the redness of the flesh. The last couple of days had been tiring, but she had kept going with her nursing through steely determination. Her patient was too fevered to be anything but docile. And the Wynne men, were mostly unskilled at domestic tasks so they kept themselves away and never dared enter the sickroom. Charlotte kept them all fed, and her friend well cared for as the fever raged.

Returning from the kitchen she spooned the beef broth into Susan, having struggled to get her upright it was a relief to see that there was the sign of her appetite returning when she didn't slow until nearly half the bowl was done.

"Now jigget, time for us to sup too!" Susan picked up little Rebecca "Wave nighty night to thy Mam." the child dutifully waved as they left the room and headed down to the kitchen.

"Sup?" Rebecca said as she struggled to get

down from Charlotte's arm.

"Yes. Some nice broth for us both and then it will be time for thee to sleep." Rebecca nodded at this and stuck the ear of her rag dog into her mouth. Her blue eyes, so like her Father's, watching solemnly as Charlotte prepared their supper. Once the bowls were safely put on the table Charlotte went to get a hunk of bread from the loaf she had baked that morning that she would use to mop up the dregs. The men would make short work of what was left so she would need to bake more come the morrow. She nearly stumbled when she turned and discovered Rebecca was right by her ankle. Arms raised and looking straight at her Godmother.

"Lot? Up!" The imperious, and precocious, child was used to being obeyed as her family were all wrapped around her little finger. Charlotte was definitely no exception.

The only time anyone had seen Charlotte smile this past year was when she was looking after the Wynne children. She obeyed the command, and juggling the child and the bread went over to the table to get them both fed. It was only after her first mouthful that Charlotte realised it was the first thing she had eaten since breakfast. Supper eaten she sat and cradled the little girl for a while, the warmth of the kitchen comfortable and peaceful. She settled into a doze.

The change in the gentle breathing of child in her arms made her realise that she had fallen asleep. Quietly she carried the girl up and put her to bed in the room that they were sharing. Briefly returning downstairs she knocked on the door to the forge and let the Wynne men know that they were able to venture into the kitchen for their own supper.

She settled herself in the chair between the bed and the window so she could sit with Susan for a bit and keep her comfortable. Susan was dozing so Charlotte dimmed the lamp to look out into the night. The full moon made the night bright as it shone on the fresh fall of snow, and the wind made dancing lace appear outside the window as it teased snow back into the sky. It was beautiful and hypnotic. She settled in to watching it for a bit whilst she waited in case Susan needed her.

The sun shining in through the window dazzled her. Rubbing her eyes, she realised she had fallen asleep in the chair. The stiffness in her joints was a rousing chorus of complaint as to why this was a foolish thing to have done. Stretching herself she tried to return some life to her legs and lower back. Glancing over she froze, safely nestled against Susan was Rebecca. Her face settled into a sweet pout. Charlotte carefully picked her up and carried the child back to her own bed. Susan's fever was still high, and fortunately she didn't wake at the disruption.

Charlotte went downstairs to begin her tasks. First she needed tea to help her overcome her discomforts, and she began to prepare the oven to bake some fresh bread. Breakfast for the hungry mouths of the household would then be the next order of business.

"Wakey, wakey." She said gently setting the tea and porridge by Susan's bedside. "I've set the bread to rise and here is yer breakfast. See if ye can manage some?" Susan stirred groggily and rubbed her eyes.

"Thank ye." Her rise was interrupted by a coughing fit. "That smells right good, I'll try and take some." Charlotte resettled the bedclothes around her patient to keep out any drafts. "Where be Becky?" Susan asked tentatively blowing on the spoonful of porridge she was bringing to her mouth.

"I'll be fetching her presently, wanted thee settled first. She snuck through in the night. I nodded off in the chair and she must've gotten lonely when I didn't come through. I put her back before getting the day started." Charlotte reassured her friend, Susan's looked wary at the news.

"Fetch her through please. It cheers me to see her playing even if I am too ill to hold her." Susan continued to eat her porridge, but her eyes kept straying to the door. Charlotte could read her friend's heart and know there would be no peace for it until she had seen her daughter.

She quietly entered and touched Rebecca's shoulder. The child turned away and snuggled deeper into the blankets.

113

"Time to get up, sleepy bones." Gently rocking the child's shoulder. Rebecca only spun deeper into the covers. "None of this now. Little Miss. Thy mother wants to see thee." She deftly untangled the infant from the bedding and took her through in her nightgown. Susan smiled to see her.

"Art ye well Becky? Sleepy still?" she asked sipping her tea. Charlotte frowned when she saw that there was still porridge left cooling in the bowl. Rebecca nodded from Charlotte's arms the pout on her face clearly indicating how she felt about being dragged from her bed. Her small hands rubbed her face repeatedly. "She looks flushed, is she fevered?" Susan's smile vanished and Charlotte looked more closely at the child. Shifting her arms she gently placed the back of her hand to Rebecca's forehead.

"A mite warm, but she is just out of her blankets" Charlotte sounded calm, but her eyes searched Rebecca's face for any of the early warning signs of the illness that had swept the village.

"I'll get thee some milk and a pretty dress and then we'll see. I'll bring her back shortly Susan." Charlotte turned and left the room, her heart racing. Dressing the little girl for the day her skin felt cooler again and Charlotte breathed a sigh of relief. By the time she had given Becky her milk and put the loaf into the oven the child was acting normally. Susan smiled when they returned, and Becky sat happily playing in her corner. Charlotte resumed her station with her knitting and gentle conversation. Below they could hear the sounds of the Wynne men about their morning routine.

The morning passed peacefully, and was rich with the smell of fresh bread that wafted comfortingly around the house once it had been taken from the oven. Susan asked for her sewing basket and Charlotte was pleased to see her feeling able to take out some small projects. They were both deeply engrossed in their works when the companionable silence was broken by a small cough. The two women froze and looked at the child in the corner. She looked up from her play and coughed again. Her lower lip began to tremble.

The next couple of hours passed with increasing worry for both women. Becky took some water, but Charlotte could tell that she was falling ill with the beginning of the fever. Her small face was too warm to the touch and slightly clammy. It was shortly after lunch that the first spots of the rash were seen on her arm, peeking out of the sleeve of her dress. Wordlessly Charlotte handed the child over to her mother. The fear of contagion mattered not, as that horse had bolted. They knew that the comfort of her mother was now paramount to the poor child. Becky whimpered piteously as the fever took hold for her small body. Charlotte hurried back and forth from the kitchen and the bedroom carrying compresses and brewing fresh teas hoping to be able to help.

"Tis my fault, she shouldn't have crept through. I'm sorry Susan, truly I am." Charlotte began to cry.

"Hush woman. I don't blame thee, she is a wilful girl and goes whither she willst. Now we are needing to keep her safe and see her through this fever." Susan struggled to keep her voice level. "I needst thee now, more 'en ever Lottie. I'm too weak to care for her alone. And thee knowst how afeared Amos is of sickness so he willnae be any use. And the lads are too small. Please. Help me Lottie." She reached out her spare hand that wasn't cradling her daughter. Charlotte grabbed it and squeezed back. Her heart breaking at the fear in her friend's green eyes.

The rash began to spread further, and the child's fever burned hotter. The two women took turns holding Becky as they used compress after compress to try and break the fever.

"Lottie!" Susan's panic made her friend spin quickly back from her intended mission to fetch fresh water. "She's taking a fit!" Charlotte froze watching the small body held in Susan's arms shuddering and shivering violently. The icy cold realisation that this was beyond her ability to help washed over her. She saw the solution as much as she hated it, but the child she had seen grow this past year who had been healing the empty space left in her heart was in dire peril. And with the devil driving she knew where she should direct his

116

carriage. She turned and ran downstairs.

"Amos! Noah!" She shouted banging on the smithy door. "Go! One of ye fetch Mistress Purkiss at once! The babe is fevered and taking a fit!" The sound of work halted immediately at her first shout and the door suddenly jerked open. Amos stood there gapping at her. "No time. I'm going back to Susan. Get thee gone. Tis most urgent! And another of thee get more water from the well." Without a further word she ran to the kitchen and grabbed the fresh jug of water and hurried back to her friend and the sickly babe.

It felt like an eternity later when she heard the heavy tread of fast feet ascending the stairs and Constance Purkiss knocked and entered in one swift movement.

"Tell me what happened." She smoothly removed her shawl and whilst listening to the jumbled words of both Susan and Charlotte was undertaking her first inspection of the babe. The rash had spread further and was now across the chest and creeping up her neck. Becky clung to her mother's neck when she was allowed to following the inspection. Charlotte watched in fear and fascination wondering what spell the witch would use to cure the child. The bottles and packages that Constance extracted looked mysterious at first until she began to unwrap them. They were just normal salves and herbs. More water was fetched, and fresh cloths and the kettle set to heat for a tea.

"Won't ye just magic the fever from her?"

117

Charlotte asked eventually. Her disbelief forcing her to speak. "I thought that ye would do it that way."

Constance sighed wearily. "Nay child. There is more medicine that is needed here than witchcraft. There is a price for the craft and while this infant is sickly it is still in the realms of nature that we first seek aid. The fit sounds right bad, but I think as it this was the first, and quick passing it was just the fever burned too hot. So, with a goodly will and sound physic we can cool it and all being well, not another bout of that will we see. The child is small, but she is strong. With loving care I think she will see this pass. Now hand me that green ribband pot of salve." Charlotte wordlessly handed over the small clay vessel.

"Oh." Charlotte felt her face flushing. "I heard from old Mistress Fairley that thou were powerful and fearful. She said that thee had made dark pacts for terrible power and could bend people to do thy bidding." Charlotte's words faltered. Watching this woman gently apply a salve to a sick babe held in her mother's arms took away the illusion of evil doing that had been spun by the gossips in the village.

"I told ye, not to believe them." Susan muttered folding the stack of linens on her bed to make a pile of fresh compresses ready for her babe's forehead and settling deeper into her pillows. The fear in her eyes had evaporated once

Constance had taken charge. "She may have a skill or two that gives her ways and means that we can but guess at, and, if ye'll pardon me saying Mistress, even though she be a witch, she is a good'un. Nary a bad word have I heard from her lips nor any credible report of an ill deed by her hands has ever reached my ears. I ken that thy pain made it an easy thing to hear, as thou already feared the worst."

"Aye, there's those as will say what's on their minds e'en if it is little and all bad echoes. I take no heed if I can. I knowst my own mind and heart best. Think what thou willt. But best think for thyself. Let not others shape thee as thou knowst not what seeds they plant nor why. The truth will out in the end." Constance smoothed Susan's hair as well and quickly checked her temperature with the back of her hand..

"I'm sorry Mistress Purkiss." Charlotte mumbled feeling small and confused by the change that had arisen. In that shared moment of care and compassion she saw her loss in a different light. Constance was the woman who had held her hand and took charge when she had been lost. "I must confess, the loss had quite clouded me and I'm sorry that I took agin thee so deeply." Charlotte felt tears begin to stand in her eyes, the embers of her buried pain rekindled at the prospect of a different loss.

"Fret not. As I said, I know myself and thy opinion stung me not. I saw plain thy pain and judged thee not for it. But I thank thee for thy apology. Thou hast done a sterling job here with the Wynne family, and ye did good to call me when thou didst. Even if I did disappoint thee by not raising hell to bring forth a mighty magic to save the day." Constance smiled at her own teasing to lessen the sting. Charlotte relaxed and joined her in a smile. Together they worked to make the mother and babe more comfortable.

Later that evening while the dinner was cooking Constance and Charlotte sat in the Wynne's kitchen. The weather outside had turned even colder and a blizzard was promising to turn the night wild. Constance thoughtfully sipped at her tea, watching Charlotte as she fiddled with the napkin in front of her.

"Tis not an easy thing, to care deeply for other's kin. But I see that thou dost and that thy heart is a good one." Charlotte reddened at these words.

"Tis no matter, I find it as easy task. They are as good as kin to me. Susan has been so kind; it would never do to see them suffer and not help. And wee Becky is such a sweetling." Charlotte's voice began to crack "I don't ken what I would do if she had been taken too." She dabbed at her eyes but kept looking down.

"Aye, that is a burden ye are already near bowed down under. Tis over a year since I last spoke to ye, and out of respect of thy pain and thy wishes I kept my path from thine. But I have an inkling that it wasn't the first loss ye have suffered?" Constance's voice was even and matter of fact. Her eyes fixed on the woman sat by her.

"Nay. Not the first, but I've done what I can to make it the last. Bill has complained bitterly but I just couldn't bear it. That was the third, and the hardest. Thirds the charm I told myself. Bah." Her voice twisted in self-mockery as she said the common phrase. "Tis like feeling cursed, or like I am wrong inside. That I am not a fit vessel. The memory of that loss, and the fear it will be added to make it easier to bear the truth that I will never have that dream of a babe of my own. Waking the day after ye left me, I found it easier to think myself as stone, bled dry. Better than seeking to hope that someday it would be different. What ne'er could be could only hurt me, so I put it away. I give my love to those as are here, not those as are but a painful fancy."

Charlotte looked up and locked eyes with Constance. "I have to know. Was it truly not even a babe? Was I that badly mistook?" The pain in the depths added a strange lustre to her dark eyes. Constance held her gaze and replied steadily.

"Nay, it was no babe. A trick of the womb. And easy to be mistaken, the cruellest of tricks. It was a growth that had no substance. I've seen a few over the years and was best that it shook free so soon. Another woman I saw when I was first learning was more than halfway along when hers

121

broke free and it near killed her. Was a sack of bloody flux and by then near putrid. I'm sorry to speak so plain, but thou hast to know the truth. Ye are strong, and if willing I don't think that ye are entirely without hope." Charlotte kept her eyes on Constance's reading the sincerity there and eventually nodded.

"Hope? I don't ken how I can hope." she began to cry gently, the dam now broken in her. Constance moved around the table and placed a comforting arm around her shoulders.

"By asking for the help that is here and freely given to those in need. My skills are at thy disposal, and I think if we work together there may yet be hope. At least to try. If ye feel able." Constance squeezed Charlotte gently and returned to her seat.

"Do ye mean magic?" Charlotte's face became guarded once more. "I will have none of that. No disrespect, healing is one thing but for making a babe it is meddling beyond what is right. It might be a changeling!" Her shoulders tightened and she studied the table in close detail.

"Nay." Constance sighed. "It is not all magic. As I said to ye, there is medicine too. I ken the herbs that may help soothe the trouble that ails ye, and mayhap thy husband too. Teas and good tinctures. Nary a spell if that is thy will. Knowledge well used can do more good than a mighty magic. I too would be afeared of a changeling, if I were to meddle with the making of a child when there was no need. We don't open doors that aren't needed when we work with the craft." Constance watched as Charlotte's body slowly untensed as she accepted the wisdom of the words.

"So ye can truly help me?" the whisper of hope putting forth a sprout in what was thought to be a barren place softened Constance's irritation at Charlotte's judgemental resistance.

"Aye. We will start with a talk about thy monthlies and perhaps raspberry leaf tea. No bashfulness now, tis a natural part of what we are trying to do and may be part of the problem. And there is a tincture I can make for ye that will help strengthen thy womb. The mistletoe is good for more than just kissing under. I've harvested much this winter and will gather more now that it is needed and eventually we will see if we can get a seed to take root in the proper season."

Constance sipped her tea. Charlotte's face had gone pale and thoughtful. "Now while our patients sleep, and the menfolk are occupied we have some time. Let's begin." Constance began to gentle gather the necessary information from her new patient and as she learnt more she felt her own confidence grow that her words had not been an empty promise.

***

"Stoke up the fire Susan!" Constance called as she took off her shawl and shook the snow from it. "Fetch more hot water, Mr Bass." He scurried out of the room; the midwife was someone that he obeyed immediately.

"Now how are ye doing my beautiful Lottie?" Constance sat on the edge of the woman's bed. Charlotte Bass was already red in the face and breathing heavily. Her abdomen arising from under the covers like a small hillock.

"It… is… definitely… time!" She panted. "Not like the last time, I promise." Constance surveyed her patient.

"I agree. What think ye Susan? Tis it Lottie's time?" Susan looked over amused at the question.

"Oh, no I think she has another month left by my reckoning, it surely cannot be now?" Charlotte tried laughing at the joke, but it became a strained bellow as another contraction squeezed her body.

"Right. Let's have a look at ye." Constance quickly washed her hands in the fresh hot water that Mr Bass had provided. He had immediately fled when she quirked her eyebrow at him in the direction of the door.

After a brief inspection of the belaboured woman she judged things needed more help. "Charlotte, I think ye needs to be up and about for now. No. Don't argue with me, the babe needs a bit more encouragement to be pointing downwards. Susan lend Lottie a hand please." With a slight effort they got the heavily pregnant woman out of her bed and began making slow progress around her bedroom. Pausing when the contractions came on and Charlotte's face became purple with the exertion.

The next hour passed with a mixture of slow shuffling, frequent resting and gentle rubbing of Charlotte's lower back. As the contractions got closer Constance monitored the situation closely.

"I think it is time. Susan get the blankets ready." Susan deftly piled the required blankets near to Constance's hands. Having been through three of her own and helped at other childbeds she knew things should be done as smoothly as possible. She smiled encouragingly at her friend and went to take her hand.

Charlotte was bent over the bed and panting heavily. "Come now Lottie, ye are doing a wonderful job. Just a bit longer and then ye'll meet thy babe." Susan paused and grimaced quietly as her friend squeezed her hand tightly as another contraction came.

"Lottie. Listen good. It is time now." Constance said having examined her patient and determined that all was aligned as it should be. "When the next contraction comes ye'll need to push like the strong woman ye are. Just do it slow and natural like. Will all be good." Constance's attention was fixed on the imminent arrival. Susan mopped her friend's face and murmured similar encouragement. Charlotte barely heard them. She was focusing on the overwhelming instructions that were coming from her body. The combination of pain and other sensations making up the miracle of birth occupying her whole mind.

"One more push!" Constance shouted at her. With a mighty groan Charlotte complied and Constance caught the babe as it slipped free from the womb. Quickly cleaning it off, cutting the cord and giving the welcoming smack to the bottom the healthy cry that followed brought smiles to the faces of all the women. "Tis a girl! Ye have a daughter." Constance announced to the room.

The afterbirth came swiftly behind the babe with a few further pushes and that done Susan helped Charlotte into her bed whilst Constance swaddled the babe and presented it to the now both smiling and crying mother.

"Mistress Purkiss it is a wonder ye have worked, tis truly magical. I never thought I'd see the day that Lottie had her own babe." Susan smiled and hugged Constance.

"No. Was no magic of mine. Just tonics and herbs and a woman's will to bear the babe. Nature did the work; I was just the helper." Constance mopped her own brow pleased to see Charlotte and the babe both glowing with health..

"Thank ye, Constance, Thank ye Susan. It is a blessing and I couldn't have done it alone. Ye have been as sisters to me in this and I thank ye. And I would like to introduce ye both to my daughter. Her name will be Hope. As that is what ye gave me." Charlotte smiled and kissed her daughter.

The two friends stood and watched the scene lit by the warm glow of the lanterns. Their hearts overflowing with joy at the sight.

The Falling Child

"More Tea, Constance?" Charlotte offered holding the pot hovering in the air above her guest's cup. The first chill of winter had settled over the county and the residents of Old Bridge had begun preparing for another hard one. And as Constance was their witch and herbalist she was much in demand for those thinking forward to what might come.

"No, Lottie, thank ye." Constance waved it away, her head tilted slightly towards the fire as if listening. Charlotte paused and listened too, the crackle of the fire and the low whistle of the wind outside were all that she could detect. As much as she liked this silence she smiled at the memory of the hubbub that her family brought to the place.

"Are ye hearing something?" She asked noticing the frown on Constance's face.

"I thought I heard a child crying." Constance muttered still attentive. Charlotte froze and listened even more attentively.

"No. I can hear nary a peep. The children will be back soon, but I hear nothing the now." She shook her head at the strangeness, but she listened once more to the stillness and pulled her shawl more closely around herself. Constance returned her attention to the room.

"Tis gone now. Nowt to be afeared of. It didn't bode ill for thee. It is far off that I hear the echo." Constance patted her friend's hand. "I'll be away I think, I've another a small errand that must be done before the sun goes down and I've idled away enough time today, as cosy as it is." As she gathered her basket the door burst open with the excited chatter of Charlotte's children and the sudden gust of cold air made the fire dance and a shower of ash to swirl from the grate.

"Mama, Mama, we are back! We nearly brought home another brother, but he had to stay. He was very sad." Hope hurried around the room to get to the fire, rubbing her hands together her face glowing with the chill. Jonathan huddled alongside her his mittened hands held towards the flame, but unlike his sister not shedding any layers to feel the warmth. William Bass, their father closed the door and nodded greeting to their guest and went to kiss his wife on the cheek.

"Oh! Ye are like ice." Charlotte remarked and quickly handed her husband her cup of tea.

"Thank ye. Aye. It is right frozen out there but was a right good day. Old Hubert liked the new designs and has commissioned me to make another three pairs of the fine shoes and another pair of slippers for his lady!"

"Old Hubert! Fie on ye. How can ye be so disrespectful to the Viscount?" Charlotte was shocked "Ye knows that this will be a good deal of business, there are those as watch what he does. It is never long after he gets thee to make something that more than one of our neighbours is found to be enquiring what style or colours it was that 'Old Hubert' as ye call him has asked for when he gave thee another commission."

"Aye. Tis true, when the Viscount has deigned to buy shoes from me the parish will be agog to see if they can have matching footwear. And I say the more the merrier, but I will not bow to him under my own roof, even if I do bow to him under his." William took his coat off and went to help his son who was starting to put the mittens closer to the fire in the hope of warming himself, the wool was only just starting to catch.

"Now what was this about another brother?" Charlotte asked, Constance paused in the action of putting on her shawl. The domestic tableau warmed her heart and the strange topic of conversation was one that intrigued her.

"At the hall, there was a boy who wanted to run away. We played with him in the garden for a bit and he begged us to let him come and live with us. But a bigger girl came and made him go back in. He was crying and begged and begged us to come back again. Which we promised to do when we may. Which I hope that ye let us as he was kind. There was a very big stick and we made a dog fetch it and then Dada took us off home again. He was very pale, the boy not the dog, the dog was a sort of red-y colour with blue eyes. He liked chasing the stick." Hope chattered away, Constance felt a gentle pricking sensation in her fingertips when the girl mentioned the boy crying and begging. She glanced over at William.

"There's not been a child at the hall for years. I wonder who it might be?" Charlotte said as she began to gather the tea things.

"Oh, that is Old Hu... the Viscount's grandson. Sad business. His son and his son's wife passed away a few months back and he only learnt of this recently, some terrible accident it was. And he has taken the boy in as his only heir. Nice enough lad I hear but has an odd name, Sin something. He said it was. That is the reason he wants more of the shoes. Aye the boy was a bit pale, when I took his measure, but that is indoors life for thee. These nobles don't see the sun unless it suits them."

William had finished with only a minor struggle taking off his own son's layers and hugged him close as he knelt by the fire while telling the tale. Seeing the women watching him and smiling at his care of his son, he coloured a little and quickly stood. Ruffling his son's hair he made his excuses about needing to start marking out the leather while the light lasted and went to his workshop.

Constance and Charlotte exchanged a knowing glance. Constance made her goodbyes, her mind occupied by the thought of this tragic child and his mysterious plea to be taken away from the manor. The echo of the crying child she had heard seemed to have found its source.

"But why?" St-John begged as Mary dragged him back into the side door of the hall. "I just want to play. Grandfather is so mean; I am sure he hates me and Grandmother is always in her room and forgets who I am most days. Those children seemed nice. Since I can't go back to the Forest house why can't I go with them?" He only gave minimal resistance as Mary's grip was firm and she seemed almost as scared as he was.

"Ye aren't well Master Sin - jun. Ye knows that Doctor Blackthorn would tan my hide if he knew I'd let ye go running around in the cold with those village children. And the Viscount has nae hate for ye, he is still all a grieving over Alfred, yer poor departed Da." St-John nodded, it had been a significant shock to his grandfather. They had been travelling but had only made it as far as his mother's family estate where the tragedy had befallen his parents.

It had been several months after their deaths that Eloise's family, the Pettirays, had decided to return St-John to the Makkary family. They had been uncertain of how to break the news to Viscount Old Bridge of what was generally referred to as 'the tragic incident' that had taken the young couple. St-John was also grieving but in his own way. His parents had been exciting but erratic figures and this trip was to have been the most time that they had really spent together. He

132

had overheard them saying that they were preparing to send him away to school after their trip. It had left him confused and uncertain if they actually wanted him at all.

Mary hurried them both into the nursery and swiftly put away St-John's jacket. "Now sit thee there and get on with thy reckoning, or summat." She went to bustle out of the room but was prevented by the figure now blocking the doorway.

"Doctor Blackthorn." Mary bobbed a quick curtsey. "Just fetching Master Sin-John a cup of tea. Does ye want any?" She kept her eyes fixed resolutely on the floor between them. He observed her carefully through his delicate glasses, his mouth working silently as if he was chewing over what he had heard.

"No. Mary. I don't. I also have told you before that Master St-John is not to have tea in the afternoons. You may bring him a warm cup of water with the tincture that I blended, but no tea!" His reedy voice carried across the silent nursery and St-John sighed heavily.

"Must I Doctor Blackthorn? The tincture makes the water go such an odd colour and it tastes most unpleasant. I am not feeling at all unwell I promise." St-John attempted to reason with his Grandfather's physician.

"Indeed you must young Sir. Your humours are most shockingly disturbed and only my strict diet, medicaments and treatments will see you

returned to full health." The almost skeletal figure
of the doctor crossed the room, Mary bobbed
another curtsey and made her escape not daring to
look back. "Now sit by the window so that I can
examine you again." The old man waved his hand
imperiously at the boy urging him towards the
afternoon sunlight slanting through the window.
His grey and translucent skin showed a disturbing
network of blue veins. St-John trudged his way
across the nursery. The easiest path in life lay
through obedience, but he resented every minute of
it. Resignedly the little boy settled himself down
for the examination.

"You are feeling somewhat cool. Have you
been outside?" Doctor Blackthorn scrutinised the
boy who squirmed under his focus.

"No. Doctor. You told me not to." St-John
looked wistfully out of the window hoping that his
lie would pass undetected.

"Hmm, you have an excess of phlegm in
your humours again, as indicated by your cooler
temperature and your obviously withdrawn
demeanour. I am afraid we must have another
letting today, if you don't improve by sunset we
must rebalance your humours." St-John jerked
upright in the chair.

"Oh, no. Please. Not another letting so soon.
I feel so very tired afterwards. I promise to be less
phlemmy. Really I do." St-John turned his attention
to the doctor. His eyes widened and despite his
normal reluctance to touch another person he

grabbed at the doctor. Doctor Blackthorn froze and stared at the young boy's hand on his own.

"Perhaps, it is too soon. But I will be watching you most closely." The doctor withdrew from the nursery. St-John slumped into the chair where Mary found him when she returned with the tinctured water. His face screwed up at the bitter taste but knowing Dr Blackthorn would be asking again he determinedly drank it all down. Mary slipped him a small piece of honeycomb to chew on afterwards.

"Are thee ready Master St-John? "Martha the housekeeper asked as she entered carrying the ledgers that would occupy their afternoon. St-John tried to pretend that he couldn't hear her and stayed reading his book. "Thou knowst that thy Grandfather wants thee to learn reckoning and know the estate and household." Martha rested the ledgers on the large table which had been designated her desk for this task

"I dinnae see Mistress Tudball as why thee art having to be a school mistress on top of being a housekeeper. Neither fitting, nor proper I shouldnae think." Mary sniffed as she continued her mending of St-John's shirt.

"And that Mary is why thee will need to learn too. Tis a kindness that I do, the Viscount and his family have been kind to me and mine and 'til he can find a proper governess or decides to send St-John to a proper school I will happily help raise the next Viscount Old Bridge to be a gentleman of good understanding and appreciation. Tis not our place to say nay to a nobleman, nor a child in need, and so I teach as well as tend to my duties. Now hold thy tongue young madam and fetch the good lamp from yonder as the light is fading for such close work."

St-John watched the interaction between the two women, it had been merely a se'ennight that he had been here, but he was already starting to see how the household operated. He had been distant from the day to day running of his parent's household, but he had picked things up and the difference from that to the whole Old Bridge estate were already enough to make his head spin. Something in their conversation pulled his attention from the book.

"Will I truly be the next Viscount?" his pale blue eyes scanned backwards and forwards between the two women.

"Aye, my lad. That is how 'Preemo Jenny chur' works, or so's as I heard thy grandfather say. Thou art the eldest, nay only, child of the only son of the current Viscount. And with thy poor father's unexpected passing, God rest him, thou willt take the role next when'er the heaven's call the current Viscount to his final rest. Not that will be for many years we hope. And that is why thou needst to learn thy numbers and how the household works." Martha fixed him with her kindly grey eyes and patted the chair next to her. St-John swallowed heavily; his eyes now serious. He slowly walked over and joined her at the table.

"I didn't realise. There is a lot to learn." He surveyed the pile of ledgers as if they would bite. "We had better get started then!" He tried to sound jolly, but the slight crack in his voice betrayed the fear that had taken root in the young boy's heart.

The afternoon passed rapidly with much careful copying, calculations and crossings out done on the nursery slate. The final entry for the day's accounts was made in the ledger in a bold but childish hand. Martha made her excuses and bid them hurry to be ready for dinner, as she had told the cook to continue with the preparations and it would soon be time for St-John to join the Viscount and Doctor Blackthorn at table. Mary began a flurry of preparations as St-John needed to be made presentable if he wasn't eating his dinner with her in the nursery.

By the time the dinner gong sounded St-John was freshly scrubbed and dressed for the dinner with his Grandfather. Mary watched him descend the main stairs until he was out of sight. She then hurried down the backstairs to get herself a seat with the other servants.

St-John pushed open the large wooden door that led into the dining room. His footsteps echoed as he walked along the cold stone floor, from his perspective the large dark wooden dining table seemed to stretch beyond the horizon. Only half

the sconces had candles lit making the paintings
and tapestries on the walls feel even more
menacing than they normally appeared. At the far
end of the table a cluster of candelabras pushed
back the darkness in a small area. The illumination
fell on the two men who now controlled his life, his
grandfather, the Viscount and Doctor Blackthorn,
his Grandfather's physician. St-John quickly took
his seat by his grandfather's side. Mr Scoggins the
butler materialising out of the shadows and
pushing his chair into place.

"Ah St-John, tell us what did you learn from
Martha today?" Viscount Old Bridge asked his
grandson. The small nod he gave to Scoggins was
sufficient to set the well-oiled wheels of service in
motion. The first course swiftly appeared at the
table whilst St-John stammered through a
summary of what Mistress Tudball had taught him
that afternoon.

"He is a good boy, Your Lordship.
Although I fear that his humours continue to be
disordered." Dr Blackthorn offered between sips of
wine. "Did you say that his mother was similarly
afflicted?"

"Charles, please call me Hubert. The weight
of the titles gets a bit much when at home at my
age. And whilst we are only now deepening our
connection, we have known each other for years. So
when we are alone, it will be Hubert and Charles
agreed?" Viscount Old Bridge sipped his wine too
and nodded for the next course to be served.

138

"Are titles very heavy Grandfather? How do you carry them?" St-John asked sipping his watered wine and nervously looking at the two adults. "I also learnt about Preemo Jenny Chur, and how I might have to be you one day."

"Ah, yes. Primogeniture. I must commend Mistress Tudball, she is giving you a more rounded education than I thought a housekeeper would be able to provide. And yes, titles do come with a certain weight, but it is carried in the spirit and the heart, not the shoulders. Noblesse Oblige! We Makkarys have been in the county for a long time and indeed my boy, you will one day have the coronet and that is why we are preparing you. I just wish the burden had been delayed longer than it will now. The devil take those Pettirays, he was too young to die! He was to be my crutch in my infirmity." Hubert Makkary's heavy fist came down on the table to punctuate his grief masked as anger. St-John and Doctor Blackthorn both jumped at the impact.

"Now, My Lord. Sorry. Hubert. Soothe yourself. It was a mystery illness by all reports. A few others were also afflicted. The letter said what it could, and I would not imagine that any blame could falling at the door of the Pettirays. Just be glad that St-John was spared." Doctor Blackthorn placated his host and signalled for more wine to be poured. "Now tell me of St-John's mother. If you would be so kind."

"She was an odd fish, but she made Alfred

happy. Her constitution was also weak, it is why they removed themselves to the smaller house in the forest on the other side of the estate. Better air, or something. Stuff and nonsense, to my mind, but she was less melancholic living in that isolated place. It made them happy, so I accede to their request." His flow of conversation was interrupted by a sudden clatter and the sound of breaking glass. The two older men turned to see St-John's right arm was flailing around wildly and the look of terror in his eyes, froze his grandfather's heart.

"Scoggins! To me." Doctor Blackthorn shouted as he arose from the other side of the table and went to secure his flailing patient. The two men laid the boy on the ground and attempted to arrest the wild motion of his limbs and to prevent him harming himself on the hard furniture and floor. The seizure passed off quickly, but he could tell the child's heart was racing. Viscount Old Bridge just sat in his chair. His eyes blank and helpless and his hand moved aimlessly on the table as he watched them tend to the boy.

"I'm sorry boy, we will have to do another blood-letting after all. Scoggins send Mary up to the nursery please. I will need her help." Doctor Blackthorn said helping the trembling child up and leading him from the dining room. "Good night Hubert. I will update you in the morning." The darkness seemed to swallow the pair as they walked away from the Viscount. Hubert sipped his wine watching the candle flames dance, his food unfinished on the plate in front of him. His eyes blurry with unshed tears.

***

"I hope ye have wiped yer feet Archie Mullens!" Mrs Ramsay the cook shouted at the assistant groundskeeper as she recognised his silhouette entering her kitchen.

"Now, Now Sara, I have taught him better than that." The soft tones of Adam Crow, the head groundsman preceded him as he entered the kitchen behind the now sheepish looking Archie. "He knows thy kitchen is hallowed ground and not to be defiled by mud, nor muck. Looks, he's e'en washed his hands." Adam made his careful way through kitchen and took his designated seat at the staff table.

Archie and the rest of the staff chuckled at the comment and the mollified cook returned to her final preparations for the main dinner. Her assistant Helen was finishing up the staff food and was keeping a watchful eye on Mrs Ramsay for any last-minute changes.

"Well and good. Now keep yerself out of the way whilst we get his Lordship's dinner out." Archie quickly slipped into his seat by his mentor and studiously observed the grain of the wood hoping that it would save him from further challenge. He brought his attention up when he felt a sudden warm presence on his other side and a soft familiar scent.

"Evening Miss Mary." he muttered, his eyes daring to lift from the table and seek out the face of the nursery maid. The corners of his mouth twitching upwards as he fought to not reveal how happy he was now she had arrived.

"Evening Archie." she responded; her smile briefly visible on her lips but remaining in her eyes. "Evening everyone." she added nodding to the rest of the staff.

"Joining us this evening are thee Mary?" Adam enquired "Is our little lordship out of thy good graces?" he smiled keeping his tone light and friendly.

"He is always in my good graces Mr Crow. And he is even in better grace as his lordship wished for the boy to join him and Doctor Blackthorn for their dinner. I gather he is to provide the estate update now having had one session with Mistress Tudball and has the knowing of it all already." Mary's rejoinder gathered smiles and few sniggers from some of the other staff.

"Aye. That he may be Mary. He is a canny lad and one day may indeed be giving the full reports. What matters is that he is learning, and that is what I urge thee to do too." Mistress Tudball's entrance had gone unremarked "So less of thy sauce young miss and see if thee can do better."

"Oh, be fair Martha, I do like a bit of sauce with my dinner." Adam re-joined which brought laughter to the table. "Now sit thee here Mistress Tudball and sing to me the praises of our little Lord St-John. It may be preaching to the choir, but I've a mind to hear how he fares. He is the spit of his late sire, gods rest him." Adam indicated the seat at his other side and with a smile and good grace she took her place. Scoggins efficiently entered and retrieved the nobles' dinner, after that the staff dinner was served and conversation sprang up around the table. The kitchen was filled with a gentle hubbub whilst those still working finished their duties. It had become a household practice, albeit an unusual one, that the cook and the butler dined apart afterwards. It was rumoured that this was so as it gave them the choice of the finer leftovers as well as the staff's dinner.

"Mary!" Mr Scoggins shouted from the door. The kitchen fell silent. His normal stuffy reserve was shaken, and the tone of panic cut through the kitchen's cheerful atmosphere. Mary freed herself from the table with some difficulty.

"What's occurred man?" Adam enquired his natural presence counteracting his lower ranking in the household with the indoor servants and enabling him to get a respectful answer.

"It is Master St-John. He has taken a fit. Mary you are to head to the nursery immediately to assist Doctor Blackthorn. I will return to his Lordship." Scoggins calmed his voice and turned on his heel to return to the dining room. The whole kitchen now heatedly debating what they knew of

St-John's condition. Mary started out of the kitchen at a run heading for the backstairs.

Reaching the nursery door, she almost collided with Doctor Blackthorn in the threshold. "Fetch my bag!" He ordered and returned to the room and began lighting the lamps and stirring up the fire. He looked over at the small figure resting on the bed. No longer shaking but now unsettlingly limp. Returning to the bedside he checked the boy's pulse; his heart was still fast, but it was no longer as frantic. Hearing a noise behind him he waved his hand impatiently. "Bring it over here stupid girl. I need the lancets and the bowl."

"I'm neither stupid, nor a girl. How is his young lordship doing?" Adam's deep voice seemed out of place in the nursery. The gravelly tones of adulthood at odds with the atmosphere of innocence.

"Who are you?" Dr Blackthorn turned on the intruder. "Why have you come here?" His demeanour becoming less guarded as the figure stepped into the lamplight. "I know you! You are the gamekeeper or something. Master St-John is resting now and will be receiving treatment once that nursemaid returns with my bag. I don't think we need any of your rural wisdom and this is not the place for an outdoors man such as yourself. Kindly depart." Mary entered with the bag and quickly handed it to Doctor Blackthorn, avoiding the unspoken reproach in his eyes that she had allowed this man to intrude into the nursery.

"I'm indeed an outdoors type, the Head Groundskeeper, in fact sir. And while I respect thy learning doctor. I am also mighty fond of young Master St-John as I was of his father, gods rest him. Therefore, I take it upon myself to be concerned for his wellbeing as the family are important to me. Intending no disrespect as it were." Adam stood his ground, observing the preparations that the Doctor was making.

"Fond or not, this is no place for spectators, and you may find it more distressing to see him treated. As I often find those with softer hearts and heads find the cure to be more disturbing than seeing someone ill. I must bleed Master St-John to rebalance his humours and I will have no interference from the likes of you." Doctor Blackthorn's voice rose to a shriller pitch as the face of the groundskeeper hardened at the mention of bleeding.

"It can't be right sir, to bleed him. He is weak enough now." Adam went to interpose himself.

"Halt Sir. I command it. I am his physician and will see him receive my treatment with no interference from a jumped-up gardener!" Doctor Blackthorn's face began to redden at this challenge to his authority. Adam suddenly felt a restraining hand on his arm as he made to press his point.

"Now Adam, tis not the time nor place to make a scene." Mistress Tudball had entered behind him. "Doctor Blackthorn has the Viscount's permission to treat Master St-John and he will not approve of any argument in his house. Especially one that interferes with a sickly child. Now, leave the Doctor to it, and we will see how the dawn finds the young man." Adam seemed braced to argue further but catching Martha's eye he deflated and simply nodded to her. Turning his back on the Doctor he let the housekeeper guide him from the nursery. The door shut behind them and he tried not to imagine the horrors of the sickbed.

"Why Adam? Why make such a scene?" she asked as they made their way back to the kitchen.

"I made a promise to Alfred, years ago when St-John was first born that come what may the boy will be as safe as I can keep him. Even agin his grandfather." Adam sounded heartbroken but determined. "We will see how he fares in the morn. And if the condition of that boy worsens then that man, Doctor or no, will have a reckoning from me." Martha kept her eyes fixed on the stairs. Under her hand she felt the powerful tension in Adam's arm. That reckoning would be mighty, so she prayed for Master St-John for both the boy's sake and for that of the doctor.

***

Constance stumped along the frosty path, her breath condensing in the air in front of her in large clouds. The day was bright but bitter and she had set off shortly after the sun rose. The fields and paths lay heavy with frost and the tree branches were coated with rime, making the day sparkle in a way that warmed Constance's heart. The depths of winter had its own stark beauty that she was coming to appreciate more now that the first hints of white were creeping into her own hair.

The day was still and bright and she approached the hall with the sun beginning to skim higher over the forest. The dark empty branches of the trees lined the path and seemed to her mind to be clustering together against the chill. She made her way to the kitchen door where she was guaranteed a welcome. Any Witch knew that the main door of a grand house was always a risk not worth taking, even when on official business. Scoggins never approved of her and so the servant's door was the safest route.

"Mistress Purkiss, tis a pleasure to see thee. Take a seat and I'll make thee a cup of something." Constance smiled at Mrs Ramsay's greeting.

"Much appreciated Mrs Ramsay it is a bitter, but beautiful day out there." She rubbed her hands to restore some heat to them, the warmth of the kitchen evoking a welcome pain as the chill was leeched from her flesh.

The ritual of minor pleasantries began and the exchange of news between the hall and the village flowed freely. Information being the vital lifeblood of a community. Constance pretended surprise to hear of the arrival of the grandson. And appropriate sympathy at the associated rumours about the loss of his parents, and his poor health. That news had already spread across the parish, and she had heard it more than once since the Bass children's version. The details of the illness of the boy however were fresher and her special senses confirmed that it was connected to her fearful premonition.

"I've come to see Viscountess Old Bridge, I have a thought she would be out of the balm that I made around now." Constance gestured to her basket. "Is there anyone else who is in need? Shall I see the child?"

"Oh, no. We are mostly in fine fettle. And whilst I think thy care would be most welcome for the young Master I fear that his care is the sole purview of Doctor Blackthorn. He takes badly to any tampering with his methods." Mrs Ramsay confided to Constance, glancing around to be sure that none could overhear them. "I think he is a quack, but he was the physician to an old friend of his Lordship's and was highly thought of at court, or so tis said. Which shows to me all the sense that they have. Which is to say none."

Constance smiled her agreement but said nothing more. She made her excuses and with Mrs Ramsay's blessing saw herself up the staff staircase to the bedchambers. The way familiar to her after a few years of support and care to the ailing Lady Angeline Makkary. Knocking on the door she waited until it was opened from within and she was welcomed with a smile.

"Ah, I thought we might see thee soon." Maggie greeted her. Maggie was her ladyship's chambermaid and now also her private nurse. "That balm is beginning to run out. She gets to move so little; it does ease her pain from laying and sitting so much." Constance dipped her hand into her basket and proffered the new clay pot.

"I know she needs it, so I keep her in mind and thought it was time for another visit. How is she faring?" Constance asked looking around the room. The Lady Angeline was asleep in her chair by the window, wrapped up in a cosy looking blanket.

"She had a rough night. The pirates were abroad again, and she would have none of my reassurances that we weren't at sea. She only settled down when I let her have one of the old swords by her bed. Thank heavens they are mostly blunt. But it was near dawn, before she calmed enough to settle." Maggie suppressed a yawn. "She can't help it. Some days she is her old self, and others, it is the fear that takes away her sense and we can barely keep her from running wild with the dark fancies that take her." The fondness and the pain that suffused the old woman's features touched Constance's heart.

"Ye've grown right fond of her over these years I can see. Ye are very good to her." Constance commented taking the seat that Maggie offered her as they settled in for the catch up.

"Aye. I've known her since we were both small. I was a maid at her father's house she has a few years on me, but we became close despite the difference in our birth. She begged for me to come with her when she married, and I've stayed by her side ever since. It grieves me so to see her disappearing like this. She is less herself as the months pass and she forgets things. She sometimes confuses St-John for Alfred, God rest him, but that is less harm than reminding her that he is gone." Maggie sniffed as her eye's moistened at the thought of their shared loss.

"Aye. Tis the hardest, cruellest thing. I've no cure for the wandering mind, it resists both magic and medicine. When the soul goes adrift it cannot easily be anchored. All we can do is ease her days and nights. Shield her from the pain. Though tis a heavy burden on those who love her." Maggie nodded at the words; Constance rested a gentle reassuring hand on that of the kindly woman. "I do have one other thing to offer. If ye'll take it. I have made her a comforter, that will soothe the worst of her fears, and help give her quieter sleep and fewer dreams. Even if it will not slow the disease it will lighten thy burden at night. I would only use it when she is struggling most, the magic is woven into it, but it will wear out over time. Nothing lasts forever." Constance unfolded the fabric bundle from her basket. The symbols that she had embroidered onto it to focus and bind the magic standing out bright against the gentle cream of the cotton. A mixture of relief and concern crossed Maggie's features as she hesitated before raising her hands to receive it.

"Thank thee. Mistress Purkiss. I'll keep it safe for times of need. Does it need aught else to work? The magic I mean?" Maggie nervously took the fabric and looked at it fascinated by the possibility.

"No. It is part of the charm. It needs no prompting and is not harmful. Just place this over her and soothe her, and this will aid thy care." Constance reassured the older woman.

"Maggie? Is that you?" the sleepy voice of Angeline Makkary interrupted them.

"Aye, my Lady. What can I do for you?" Maggie went over to her mistress's chair.

"Oh, nothing I just heard a voice and wasn't sure where you were. Oh Hello. I know you don't I?" Angeline Makkary tried stirring from her chair when she saw they had a guest.

"Aye my Lady, it is Mistress Purkiss. Come to see how you are." Maggie reassured her. Angeline's eyes struggled to fix on the figure of her visitor. Constance moved closer to make it easier for her and to observe her patient more closely.

"Tis a pleasure to see thee again Lady Angeline. How art thou faring?" Constance settled herself by the chair and listened to her as she talked about whatever crossed her mind. Nodding and smiling she encouraged the Viscountess to continue on with her chatter, she was tired but carried on for some time.

"Oh, that was pleasant, but I am so very weary. Pray excuse me Mistress Purkiss but I find that I am requiring a nap." without any further comment Lady Angeline shut her eyes and settled down into the chair.

"Sleep well my Lady." Constance responded and withdrew to the other side of the room with Maggie to make her own farewells. She had confirmed that there was no additional care she could offer. Easing the body when the mind takes flight was all she could accomplish.

Letting herself out into the corridor she paused for a moment to allow her eyes to adapt to the dimness after the sunny bedroom. Suddenly she found herself nearly tumbled over by a dark figure hurrying along the hall.

"Clumsy woman. Look where you are going!" a petulant reedy voice cut through the darkness. As Constance's eyes finished adjusting she made out the elderly and stick thin man who had bumped into her.

"My pardon sir, but it was thee that walked into me. Not the other ways around. I'll thank thee kindly to speak more fairly as the fault is thine." She kept her voice even, refusing to be cowed by someone who wished to blame another for their own thoughtlessness.

"Who are you?" Dr Blackthorn enquired his eyes squinting at her as he attempted to place her.

"You aren't a servant here are you? How dare you speak to me with such cheek? What were you doing in her ladyship's bedchamber? Come on speak up. You seemed able to talk for yourself before. Out with it!" His voice rising in pitch rapidly as he vented his frustration at being challenged.

"I am Mistress Purkiss of Old Bridge and giving my care to the Viscountess. Thou must be Dr Blackthorn. I will bid thee good day, as I have no wish to linger here." Constance went to leave but found his hand grabbing her arm.

"Wait right there." Dr Blackthorn started but suddenly released her and muttered sharp curses as he shook the pain from his hand. The door to Lady Angeline's bedroom opened abruptly.

"What is all this commotion. Are you okay Mistress Purkiss?" Maggie asked. "Oh, Doctor Blackthorn I didn't see you in the shadow." This brought a tight smile of vindication to Constance's mouth and a twisted grimace to Dr Blackthorn's.

"You know this, woman?" He enquired wishing to disprove Constance's story.

"Yes, she is a great help to Lady Angeline and has been visiting to offer her help." Maggie offered seeming confused that there was any doubt that this was the case.

"Oh. Thank you Miss Wood. My apologies Mistress Purkiss." Doctor Blackthorn chewed out the apology as if it were leaving a bitter taste in his mouth.

153

"Thank thee Maggie, Good day Doctor Blackthorn. Farewell both." Without further ado Constance left the scene. She had seen enough of Doctor Blackthorn to know she trusted him less far than she could throw him. There was more to be done to help the sick child, but she was uncertain how to get through the barrier that the Doctor represented.

***

"And where do thee think thou art going?" Adam asked the little pair of legs that he found sticking out from under a hedge. With a firm but gentle hand he pulled the child out from his ineffective hiding place.

"Let me go! I want to go!" St-John shouted as he felt himself being dragged mercilessly backwards.

"Ah, Master St-John. What an unexpected pleasure. Enjoying the freedom of the estate on this fine afternoon?" Adam deliberately kept his tone jovial as the child's tear streaked face threatened to break into a fresh deluge.

"I'm not. I've had enough. I want to go and live in the village, or the forest or anywhere. I've had enough of Doctor Blackthorn. I know I'm ill, but I'd rather be ill than have him cure me. I'm sure he is making me worse." St-John looked around as if trying to find an escape route.

"Oh, child. Tis a cruel hand ye have been

154

dealt. Come here. I cannae chase ye if ye make a break for it, but I promise ye that I'll aid ye the best I can." Adam pulled the child into a gentle hug and felt the small body tense at first and then relax into the offered comfort. "I knew yer Da, for many years, and we were right close. I'm sorry that I didnae get to know ye sooner. But now he is gone I'll be here when ye need a shoulder to cry on." St-John could hear the tears thickening in the man's voice and it made him feel safer to know that this man had been his father's friend.

"Why does he hurt me so?" St-John begged. Trying to find reason in the confusing situation.

"Tis his way, his learning tells him that the pain is part of the cure. And it can be but not always, sometimes it is just more pain and not healing. I think he cannae tell the difference anymore. Blinded by his own knowledge to what his wits would tell him had he but the ear to listen." Adam patted the child's back hoping that his words would ease some of the burden. They stood for a few moments in silence, letting the still of the woods enter into their hearts.

As they separated, both man and boy paused when they heard a sudden crashing noise that grew louder and was joined by a voice that was screaming incoherently. St-John pushed his hand into the larger and slightly dirty hand of the Head Groundskeeper as they both slowly moved towards the sound. A short while later they found Lady Angeline in a clearing waving around a large stick and thrashing bushes as if she thought they contained something dangerous.

"My Lady! What ails thee?" Adam tried to get her attention. When she saw him, she snarled and waved the branch at him but continued to attack the undergrowth. "Stay back St-John. It seems that she is out of her wits right now, best to keep thy distance." Adam tried to slowly approach the manic Viscountess but wasn't able to get close to her. He fell back and was considering his options when he was startled to hear St-John burst into song behind him.

The boy's voice was weak, but the tone was good. It was a simple nursery rhyme about the coming of the evening and the list of things that a good child would do before going to bed. Lady Angeline's frantic efforts began to slow and eventually stopped. She slowly turned towards the source of the music, the stick in her hand now hanging loose at her side. She began to join in the song, the stick falling to the ground unheeded as she began to skip towards her grandson.

St-John fixed his eyes on her and carried on the song, beginning again when it reached the end. Adam watched astounded as the elderly woman tried moving like a little girl holding out her skirts as if she were daintily treading a measure. St-John offered her his hand and she took it, carrying on the song. She turned and smiled at Adam and offered him her other hand. St-John nodded encouragingly. Adam quickly took her hand so she couldn't pick up another stick and he tried to join in. His singing voice was rough, but the familiar simple songs from childhood were soothing and the wish to get her ladyship home safely overcame his embarrassment.

Hand in hand the trio began their walk back to the hall, shifting to nursery rhyme after nursery rhyme to maintain the magic effect on the ill woman.

***

"It is plain Hubert that this quack of a witch isn't helping your wife. I think you should also turn her care over to me immediately." Doctor Blackthorn stood in the library. Viscount Old Bridge sat in his chair. The fire crackled in the silence.

"I don't know Charles. Mistress Purkiss has been very important to Angeline for a few years. She might be a little bold, but on the whole she seems to give my wife some modicum of peace." The Viscount wrung his hands.

"She is not trained, she has some herbal knowledge, but I doubt it is more than luck and being calm that has worked so far. In fact, I wonder if she has not allowed a degeneration in her Ladyship's condition. Look how today went with her being brought back from the forest by your Head Groundskeeper, another disreputable sort might I add. No Hubert. I must insist. For the good of your family I must take over her care. The lower members of this household seem not to know their place." Doctor Blackthorn stood over the Viscount looking as stern as he could muster.

"Let me sleep on it Charles. I will give it some thought and let you know in the morning. I don't think Angeline responds well to change. I'll have to think it over." Hubert tried to make his voice firm, but the doubts that he was struggling with made it difficult for him to retain any form of certainty. With the death of his son, his wife's worsening condition and his grandson's illness he was feeling the weight of his years as well as his title.

"I will bid you goodnight your lordship." Dr Blackthorn continued to look sour, "I have faith that you will see the sense of my proposal. Until tomorrow." Dr Blackthorn made his way out leaving the Viscount to contemplate his options.

Climbing the stair Dr Blackthorn had a flash of inspiration. The Viscount was a good man, but very weak willed when it came to his wife. "Maybe a demonstration would help him see the benefits?" He muttered to himself as he paused at his bedroom door.

Shortly afterwards he slipped out of his room with his medical bag in hand. Knocking on her ladyship's bedroom door Maggie opened it a crack. The light inside framing her as she occupied the space preventing his entry.

"What can I do for you Doctor Blackthorn?"

her tone remained polite but wary. "It has been a most trying day and her ladyship is still a little unsettled." Doctor Blackthorn placed a hand on the door and forced her to retreat so he could enter the room.

"That is why I am here. To see how her ladyship fares under professional stewardship." He moved across to the bed where Lady Angeline was lying in a light doze. Her nightgown was freshly laundered and the stark whiteness seemed to make her face look even more pale than it had been that afternoon, her eyelids twitched occasionally.

"Has Lord Hubert agreed to this?" Maggie asked her disbelief clear.

"His Lordship and I have recently discussed the matter." He waved her off dismissively and began his inspection of his new patient. "Pray tell me about her ladyship diet? I fear her humours are mostly cruelly imbalanced to have her wits so deranged." He sat on the edge of the bed listening to the reluctant litany of foods that Maggie had fed to Angeline recently.

"As her ladyship has no previous history of melancholia I suspect that this is most likely a case of *melancholia adusta,* this means she has unnatural burnt black bile afflicting her brain. This is merely a temporary *paraphrosyne*. That is derangement to a layperson such as yourself. I fear her liver is overly hot and has resulted in this most serious decay. I think I may have a cooling tincture that will begin to reverse the effects." He removed the tasteless rustic looking blanket that the nurse had draped over his patient and turned to unpack his bag onto the bed, the box of tinctures being kept secure at the bottom. His roll of phlebotomy tools fell open as he put them down, the shiny glint of his various lancets and a scarificator caught in the lamp light. Lady Angeline screamed.

"Doctor Blackthorn, duck!" Maggie shouted as she leapt backwards. Doctor Blackthorn was too slow and the wild arc of the blunt sword caught his arm as he attempted to retreat from the bedside. Lady Angeline had grabbed her comfort sword left behind from the last dream of pirates and was waving it at the retreating doctor.

"Pirate! Murderer! Call the Captain! We are boarded! We are boarded! Enemies at Starboard!" Her voice filled the room and Doctor Blackthorn stumbled away from her onslaught only saved from another blow as the sword caught in the bed curtains as her ladyship attempted to pursue him.

"Lady Angeline! Calm yourself. I am a doctor not a pirate. Maggie help me. I think she has broken my arm!" The Doctor scuttled away from the angry noblewoman who was defending her ship from this perceived threat.

"I think you had better leave Doctor. I will never calm her while she can still see you. I'll gather your things. But until the 'pirate' is gone she will continue to pursue you. Go quickly. I'll convince her you jumped overboard." Maggie remained calm, she had seen worse attacks and for less reason. She suppressed a smile at Angeline's spirit to defend herself from such an attack, which had left her struggling tangled in the bedcurtains.

Doctor Blackthorn nodded and fled. Pulling the door shut behind him he stumbled into the Viscount who was approaching from below.

"My apologies Hubert, there has been a misunderstanding and I find myself somewhat inconvenienced. I will discuss it with you in the morning. Good night." Dr Blackthorn quickly disappeared into his bedroom shutting the door and muffling the slowly diminishing sounds of outrage from the other bedroom.

***

"So, he was kicked out the next day?" Constance asked sipping her tea. The unexpected arrival of Adam Crow at her door was less of a shock than the news that he brought.

"Aye. Doctor Blackthorn has been evicted and good riddance. He left with quite the flea in his ear. The Viscount took badly to the old Doctor's presumption. But that means that young Master St-John is without any care, and I hoped that ye might lend him yer aid. Her ladyship is quite recovered, Maggie said to thank ye for the blanket. It must be right cosy as apparently it soothed her ladyship right off to sleep even after the Doctor's fright."

"Of course I'll help. I must come along to the hall at once. I will bring some things, but I will need to know more of what ails him." Constance

161

began to pack her basket. "The sky is looking threatening. We must hurry, a storm is coming and the snow. It feels all itchy. I like it not." She gathered her shawl and they headed out into the late afternoon.

"How didst thee know to come to me Mr Crow?" Constance asked as they passed through the village on the way to the hall.

"Ah, please call me Adam. Tis well known in these parts that thee were here to pick up where Mother Beecham, god rest her, stopped. I saw thee at the funeral, but I hadn't the heart to speak, and now the need comes, speak I must. It will not surprise thee that Mother Beecham was a great aid to me a long time ago. So I know where to look for help when the need is greatest." Adam kept his eyes firmly fixed on the path. Constance could feel the unspoken parts of his story. Hints of loss and of grief spun around him like a fog, but now only memory and not the crushing weight it once was, with at the heart of it the thread of a promise binding him still.

"Ah. Aye. She was a mighty help to many. We all miss her." Constance nodded. They continued on to the hall. The clouds scudding across the sky bringing an early sunset to the winter afternoon. They walked closer together to guard against the increased buffeting of the wind. It was with great relief they reached the hall just as the snow began to fall. An unexpected peal of thunder shook the heavens as they reached the threshold. Hurrying inside with a wild flurry of snow they startled Mrs Ramsay in her kitchen.

"Tis a wild one out there." She remarked "Come to the fire and warm thyselves. I don't need told why ye have come, that old curmudgeon has gone, and someone must look to the sick, and who else but our good witch."

"Hush now. Tis not proper to call her such. She is just a wise woman." Archie Mullens interposed from his corner.

"Why not Archie. Witch I am. And Good too I hope. Both at it and in my heart. So, I fear not the name, even though other try to shame with it. A witch as thy friend is the surest way to have fewer enemies. At least for long." Constance chuckled; the flush of embarrassment sent him scurrying from the kitchen.

Constance draped her shawl to dry by the fire and left Adam thawing himself and receiving praise from the staff for seeking out help for the young master. Heading up the stairs Constance passed her normal port of call and proceeded to the nursery. There she found Mary and St-John reading together by the fire.

"Mary. Master St-John." She spoke after she entered. Her sudden appearance from the shadows startled them both.

"Can I help you Madam?" Mary asked rising to greet her "Oh, tis thee Mistress Purkiss. I couldn't tell thee from the devil in this gloom." She bobbed a quick curtsey but became more informal when she saw who it was.

"I think thee wouldst know the devil better as I have fewer horns." Constance retorted. "Anyhow. I have come as I hear that our young Master St-John has recently rid himself of a meddlesome physician, but mayhaps is not in as fine fettle as would be wished." Constance smiled at the boy. He remained solemn looking and stayed in his seat.

"I'm fine thank you. I need no help." His response was polite but hid the fear that Constance could almost taste in the air. Another crash of thunder broke the silence. His arm began to tremble.

"I knowst thou art a strong lad and have seen much ill. But thou canst trust me if thee wishes. I will do thee no harm." Constance span an aura of calm to try and soothe him.

"I've had enough of medicines. They taste foul and they just make me worse, leave me alone." St-John stumbled to the window and stared out into the swirling snow. The gardens were illuminated by a flash of lightning and a rumble of thunder which made him shiver all the more.

"Ah, that is the difference. I'm not just bringing thee medicine Master St-John. I am bringing thee magic." Constance walked over to join him. "Watch!" Constance pointed out the window. A fork of lightning struck a tree at the edge of the forest. The afterglow dazzled him and he gasped. Looking at Constance she seemed to briefly glow the same colour as the lightning.

"Magic?" He whispered. His eyes large and round. The trembling stilled.

"Aye. Magic. It comes from being a witch, and as thy friends will testify a good one. Now Mary, fetch us all some tea if ye would be so kind, and we can have a chat about what ails young Master St-John." Constance walked away from the window and settled herself on a chair by the fire. Mary and St-John exchanged open mouthed stares, until Mary nodded quickly, bobbed a curtsey and fled to make the tea.

The afternoon passed quickly into evening and Mary arranged for Constance to have a guest bed made in one of the spare servant rooms. The suggestion from St-John that they ask the Viscount for a proper guest room had quickly been rejected by Constance as too much fuss.

The next day Constance returned to the nursery. The storm had passed, and the day was bright and clear.

"Wrap up warm the pair of ye. I want to take ye for a short walk. There is a sight I think ye will want to see, and a walk will do ye both the power of good." Constance refused to be drawn on anything else despite their repeated pleas for more information.

The snow was quite deep after last night's storm but they were able to make headway, cutting a deep swathe through the fresh snow. Constance led them directly towards the woods at the edge of gardens. As they approached the tree line they could see the target that she was leading directly towards. It was a large oak, and despite the advanced winter was showing some signs of greenery. It was host to a large branch of mistletoe.

"See there." Constance pointed to the mistletoe. "Next to the mistletoe, the darkness there. That is charring." And they could see that this was the tree that had been struck by lightning last night, the fire had been short lived. "This mistletoe is even more powerful as it is the embodiment of that lightning. It will make a potent potion that will keep thy falling sickness at bay. I will now harvest it and set to work." She pulled a silver sickle from her basket. "Leave me to my work, but rest assured thou will be well soon." St-John ran forward and hugged her legs before running back and grabbing Mary's hand and dragging her away back to the house. Obedient to the witch's instructions. Mary looked both scared and bit bewildered.

"Have they gone?" A voice called from behind the tree.

"Aye Adam. They are well away. Bring out the ladder." Constance turned and smiled at the Head Groundskeeper.

"Is it truly made from lightning? Didst thou truly make it strike this tree?" Adam sound both skeptical and hopefully, the wonder lingering in his voice.

"Aye and nay. I helped a little, but the storm was of its own making. Mistletoe is a symbol of lightning, but this branch has been there for a goodly time. I just needed to give that boy more hope. The potion that I will make from this is medicinal, but his trust in its magic will help him more. His heart has been wounded so we can heal it with a little bit of wonder as well." Constance mounted the ladder and began harvesting the mistletoe.

The Good Host

Last night's storm had torn some trees from the ground and Adam had risen early to repair the damage to his property, but now he was fastening the last section of his broken fence back into place. The previously settled snows had been scattered revealing the frozen earth beneath in uneven patches. His breath billowed in frosty clouds in the still air.

The chill bit deep into his twisted fingers. The creeping rheumatism had taken some of his speed and dexterity, but his lifelong stubbornness offset this and he kept going.

"Ho there!" Adam looked up into the smiling youthful face of the newest Viscount Old Bridge, St-John Makkary. The young lord adjusted his seat in the saddle, the horse jostling as he gently pulled on the reins. Although a few years had elapsed since his grandfather had passed he still kept up the personal visits on his most valued tenants, eager to properly fulfil his obligations.

"Good day yer Lordship." Adam nodded to his youthful landlord. Picking up his stick the old man hobbled towards the gate.

"I see you have been fixing fences. Has anything else been put awry in the storm?" St-John leant forward across the neck of the horse who was investigatively sniffing the fence. His face glowing with both the cold and some honest concern. "You should have waited, and I would have sent someone to help you. I am sure Archie would have been happy to lend a hand."

Adam squinted up at his former employer. "I ken he would, he's a good lad, and knows a fair bit that I taught him. So many thanks and all yer lordship, but when I can't fix my ain fences ye can put me to bed with a shovel." St-John's laugh captured the perfect balance of amusement and exasperation.

"You sir are a cantankerous old codger, but as we agreed at your retirement you are the master of your own domain within this cottage and its grounds. Therefore, I cannot force you to accept my help, even though it is freely offered. If there is ever anything you require you only need to ask for it. I still don't understand why you wanted this small isolated place as your grace and favour lodging. There are so many cottages nearer the hall. Are you sure there is nothing I can do?" St-John made to dismount but Adam waved his hand dismissively.

"I thankee most kindly yer lordship but I am most firm. I am self-sufficient and this place has fond memories for me that I like to be alone with.

Now I am put out to pasture. I've done the lion's share of the tasks and by my own hand. There is just this one final bit to be done and after that I will take a sit with a cup of tea and enjoy the simple knowledge that I did for myself." Adam hobbled slowly towards the door and collected the strewn mistletoe branches from where they had become tangled in the bare bushes by his door. Those on the ground were left where they had fallen. The berries were long gone, but the distinctive shape of the sprigs caught St-John's eye.

"Hanging Mistletoe? So late in the winter. Yule has long passed. Why are you still hanging that? Not seeking to kiss any visiting maidens are you?" St-John chuckled at his own joke, the thought of his old Groundskeeper with any woman was just ridiculous.

"Nay, yer lordship, tis not for kissing. I put this up until Bride's feast as a sign that my home is hospitable for all. Be they human or be they fey, all are welcome who enter with good intent." Adam re-tied the bundle of twigs and secured them to the nail that he had fixed there for this very purpose.

"Fey?" St-John laughed again. "I didn't know that you thought of the elves as likely visitors. I've not heard tales like that since I was a child. They all sound so foolish now."

"What sounds foolish to a man in his prime may sound wisdom to a child, and when ye reach my age ye judge less the fools, as they see things that us busy men are too blind to allow into our fancy. There are fewer hard certainties now at my age, the world is a strange place and I no longer pretend to myself that I know all its secrets.

So, I make space for that doubt and don't allow it to hold court over my senses. Anything which speaks to kindliness and does no harm can be but wise foolishness. And better a wise fool than a foolish wiseman. And the fey smile on fools." Adam nodded as the mistletoe bundle hung firm after he tugged the string a few times to judge its strength.

St-John shivered as a fresh chill breeze ruffled his hair, he paused as he caught his hand in the unconscious act of crossing himself and gave Adam a wry smile. "As I said before you are the unchallenged master in your own home, and I am glad to hear that you are hospitable to whomsoever may call upon you with good intent. I will carry on my rounds and bid you good day." St-John gathered his reins and urged his mount into a gentle trot. Adam watched him go before making his slow way into the cottage.

The rumble of an approaching cart roused Adam from a dose, curious he went to his window and peered out. The afternoon sun was starting to touch the tops of the trees, casting long shadows from a sky shading to lavender. The clouds that began to streak the sky were echoes of the previous night's display, but Adam knew that there was no bad weather coming. The ache of the cold was in his bones, but there was not a sign of the twinge that had warned him of the previous storm. Unable to make out who these unexpected guests were he headed for his porch.

"Adam Crow? Are ye at home? Put the kettle to the fire, ye've got guests!" A strong female voice called out to him. He pulled the front door open to see who was there.

"Is that Mary? Forgive me, Mrs Wynne now." Adam smiled at his old colleague as she disembarked from the wagon. "What brings ye all this way?" Adam kept one hand on the lintel as he waved to his visitors.

"Aye, tis Mrs Wynne. But Mary still or I will be forced to call ye Mr Crow. And I know that puts ye into a right temper, which is not the mood I want for my visit. And ye've more than just me to contend with as well. I've got Mistress Purkiss too!" She bustled her way down the path and gave the old man a quick hug. "His Lordship has asked that I give ye some more supplies. He said that ye were expecting some fine guests?" Mary looked around the room as if they were hiding.

"Ah, St-John. That boy, he is having a jest. But I'll not turn down the vittles, nor the company. This morn I told him that I marked my home with mistletoe to show the fey that they are most welcome. A different type of lord and lady than ye have at the hall!" Adam shook his head as he chuckled.

"If it were for anyone other than ye Adam I would turn around and take this back and give this lordship a right scolding." She shook her head at the ridiculousness of her master's order.

"Ye are no longer his nursemaid Mary, that would not be wise." Mistress Purkiss chided as she joined the group at the threshold of the cottage. "Although Mr Crow here shows more old wisdom than his lordship. Having the fey feel kindly to thee is ne'er a foolish thing." She gently brushed her fingers against the bundle of mistletoe twigs.

"Please Mistress Purkiss, Adam is my name and all that I feel is needed. Pray come in and have some tea. Tis the least I can do to repay the foolish errand Master St-John sent thee both on." Adam beckoned for them to enter. Mary paused and shouted back to the cart driver. "Unload the cart! I'll open the kitchen latch for ye." She slipped past Adam and went to oversee the unshipping of the food into Adam's stores.

"Many thanks Adam. Twas Mary's errand that was inspired by a foolish thought but may prove to be wiser than we know. Mine errand is not from the same source, it's my own business that I attend. I had a feeling I should visit ye when Mary announced her trip whilst I was at the hall. I now see hints as to why I might be needed." She dropped her voice to a close whisper. "Are they still here?" Her eyes darting around the cottage as she settled herself in the chair by the fire that her host had indicated.

"Aye. Well, nearby." Adam whispered back with a twinkle in his eye. "Those provisions will make a fine feast for more than just I this night."

With Mary's return the conversation returned to the storm and general news from both village and hall. Mistress Purkiss kept her senses tuned into the cottage and began to pick up more faint hints that they were not alone. When Mary announced it was time to leave she bustled out to chivvy the wagon driver to prepare for the return

trip. Mistress Purkiss held back making a deliberate
fuss over settling her shawl just so.

"Now Adam, I thankee for thy hospitality. I
see that ye are no stranger to making people
welcome, but I had such a feeling that something
was awry that I had to come and see for myself.
The storm may have passed but there is another
brewing. Guard thyself well." With that parting
warning she made her way out and was helped
into the cart by the driver. The sun was now
sinking below the tree line and the lengthening
shadows touched the cottage like cold dark fingers.
Adam waved them off and returned indoors to the
warm fireside.

***

"But Hob, I don't see why." Tom
complained as he moved the last of the sacks into
the corner of the room.

"Tis as Bill told us, we need supplies and
that old codger has more than he deserves. Did ye
not say that ye had seen that his lordship just sent
him another cart load?" Hob responded from his
chair at the table where he had finished sorting the
loot from their last raid.

"Aye hold yer tongue lad. Or I'll see yer
hold it for a mite longer." Bill slammed the door

behind him "Have ye done? All packed?" He threw an empty sack on the table.

"Nearly, just this last lot to be done and then tonight's little bit of fun and then we can hit the road. Although I don't see why we must go so soon. Winter has a month or so left, and the land is still frozen. It makes for hard beds on the road." Hob replied beginning to carefully transfer the fine silverware into the sack. Wrapping the pieces to prevent any tell-tale clanking when they were travelling.

"Tis sooner than I wanted, but that brat of a Viscount has begun doing his rounds of the estate and this place will not long pass unnoticed if he comes too close. He was sticking his nose in places after the storm and will most like be checking here soon. We want to be well gone before any sets foot in this place. So the cold ground it will be, until we can hock this haul." Bill held up one of the ornate candlesticks embossed with the Makkary crest and watched the light dance on the silver. He passed it to Hob so he could wrap it with the other one.

"But tis not right, stealing an old man's food from his kitchen. Tis not like taking some from the hall granary, or the riches off the likes of Makkary. He has more than he needs tis clear, this old house standing empty and all. But that old man in the

176

tithe cottage has done us no harm." Tom tried to reason with his companions.

"Not done us harm? Not done us harm? Ha! Was it not that old fox who turned me away, just cos he didn't like me?" Bill almost shouted. "And refused to take on poor Hob here?" His normally grey and surly face became flushed a deep red and the mouth twisted as the memory made the words taste sour in his mouth.

"I didn't ken." Tom muttered, focusing on rearranging the sacks and trying to allow the torrent of rage from his accomplices to pass.

"Ye said that he didn't give ye yer due." Hob added, his own grievance less stinging but equally happy to rehearse why it was necessary to teach the old man a lesson and take their share from his surplus supplies.

"Aye. Was true. I was the strongest and all and he refused to give me more than the others, and to tell them to do as I said. That Adam and his puppy Archie thought themselves so smart. But neither could lift half what I could." Bill carried on.

"But didn't ye say that ye barely lifted a finger?" Tom couldn't help himself, the memory of a different conversation betrayed him. He bit his lip and hoped it would not win him another belting.

"Aye, true. I decided to not give them the sweat from my brow, but that was by the by. I was still stronger, and they should have given it me, as my due. Twas about what I *could* do, not what I actually did. They would rather that I slaved for them. And Hob here, all he did was prove that the tools were shoddy." Bill went with the flow of his rant and waved at his friend for back up.

"Aye. That fork was as thin as a twig, took barely any of my weight to snap it right through!" Hob nodded and carried on with the wrapping of their loot. "And if it hadn't snapped over that rock then I would have been stuck shifting that manure all day, and that was not what I wanted." Hob and Bill nodded to each other. Tom looked between them but kept his own counsel.

"See, they are bad people young Tom, and once that beard comes in properly ye will have the sight to see people for what they are." Bill told him and watched the boy's face flush bright red at the mention of his scraggly beard. "Now rest up, we will be going a few hours after sundown. And we will need to get all we want quickly."

***

The firelight glinted in the dark red of the wine as it swirled in the glass.

"A fine enough vintage. Viscount Old Bridge really does place some value on you, if this is what he provides in jest!" The honeyed tones of Adam's principal guest filled the small cottage dining room. Adam smiled and sipped at his own glass, the remains of the sumptuous feast littering the table between them. The elegantly voiced guest gestured to the other visitors around the table in their array of shapes and strange finery. They rose quickly from their places and with murmured thanks they bowed first to their host and then to their lord before they shimmered and vanished, leaving the man and the noble elf to their after dinner conversation.

"Aye, he is a good lad. Right kind, a goodly soul. In some ways a son of my heart, even if not of my blood. The spit of his poor father, gods rest him. Looks more like him every day." Adam stared into the dregs of his wine for a moment. "I still miss him." His eye moistening with the tears that he still tried not to shed.

"You are a kind one Adam Crow." The elf watched him closely. The fascination he felt towards this mortal, who welcomed spirits into his home was clear. His eyes changed shade in reflection of this mood. "I wonder if you would be kind enough to tell me why you extend your welcome to the fey, and have shared this feast with us? I sent the others away as I sensed your heart was growing heavy, but I would gladly listen if you would unburden yourself." Adam looked up and met the eye of his guest.

"The world has not been a kind place to me at times, and the love that I found and lost twice made me see that there was a right way and a wrong way for a man to be. I choose to not be a shadow on anyone." The old man shivered at a memory long buried that stirred. "There were those as chose otherwise. When all a person can bring to others is darkness they only make the world brighter when they eventually leave it. The better ones, who even at their darkest times had kindness, were a loss whenever they go as they brought more light to everyone just by being. So, for those hearts to be snuffed out untimely was a crime."

Adam drained the dregs of his wine and set the glass down on the table. "And what of thee my lordship? I never asked my guests before why they wanted to sup with me, it seemed churlish. But thee are by far the noblest of the spirits that have accepted my shelter in many a long year. Even if it weren't for thy noble mien I sees the way the others bowed and hung on thy words and gestures. I will confess I am most curious as to why my humble table now gets graced with one such as thy fine self." Adam tried to hold eye contact but broke away when he felt the touch of the elf's mind in his own and saw the eyes abruptly change from the friendly cornflower blue to a cooler shade that glittered like the ice on the lake.

They sat frozen for a moment. The elf observed the elderly mortal closely and then abruptly laughed, the ice melting from his eyes and he returned them to a gentler aspect.

"You are a bold man, as well as an old one!" The elf's laughter continued for a moment; Adam relaxed as the atmosphere again became convivial, the feeling of threat had passed. The lordly elf rose from the table and went to stand by the fire. "You have been spoken of as a friend to the fey, and of the lower spirits for years now. A mortal who fears us not and does not seek to buy our favour by these marks is so rare. Respect is best found where it is earned, rather than when cheaply bought.

My allies amongst the local sprites spoke highly of your hospitality, and when I passed nearby on other business I felt it as a beacon in the darkness and I bethought myself to try it first-hand. I will confess, with simple gratitude, it has been most pleasing. In my longs years it is has been a rarity to find one such as yourself amongst the mortals, one who is not frightened of my kind and constantly guarding against us, it is an intriguing and most welcome oddity." He raised his glass and saluted Adam.

"I've seen more than most in my years. Spirits, sprites or mortal souls we are all the same. Although some of my kind hold that belief heresy. However I know that kindness goes not amiss whether ye have skin, scales or fur. When ye have been kissed by a ghost and loved an alchemist ye tend not to judge too harsh how others make their way in the world." Adam watched the candle flame dancing on the table.

"That all sounds most intriguing. I think there are more tales we should share. Brandy?" the elf suggested.

"I'm sorry I've none to hand my lordship. His lordship, the Viscount, sent wine, but no spirits. If ye'll pardon the phrasing."

"Perhaps I can provide? The elf suggested. "Freely given and with no obligation, but as a token of my esteem and gratitude." He gestured and a dusty bottle appeared between them.

"Aye, I'll drink more with ye, although ye have refused to tell me thy name, so I cannae thank thee directly. I trust thy offer and heartily drink to the health of the company." Adam accepted the

182

glass that the elf proffered having opened the bottle and poured measures for both of them.

"You mortals give your names far too freely, the honorifics sound stilted but they will do for now. I accept your toast and add here is to our future happiness." The glasses clinked and the fragrant brandy was sipped. The silence that settled between them only broken by a matched pair of appreciative sighs and the crackling of the fire.

"And now, freshly lubricated, I believe I have the honour to share a tale or two with ye." Adam chuckled as the elf keenly leant forward with his elbows on the table and settled in for the telling.

***

The thin sickle of the moon hung in the darkness overhead. Thousands of stars glittering like snowflakes suspended in the expanse of the winter sky. Unseen to human eyes the spirits who had shared in the hospitality of Adam's humble home danced and played both in and out of it. Passing easily through the doors and window as the invitation gave them that freedom. Their keen eyes and ears detected the approach of Hob, Bill and Tom before they had even left the forest. The more curious sprites went to investigate the approaching humans and heard what passed between them.

"Now Tom, hold yer tongue lad. Tis always a tricksy business breaking a house, especially a small one like this. But we knows it has rich pickings and the old man is lame and his hands aren't as nimble as they were. We can easily catch him out and quell him if he tries anything." Bill continued his experienced lecture on the finer points of burglary.

"But I dinnae ken why we can't just wait 'til he is asleep and raid the kitchen stores and be gone." Tom continued until a heavy hand abruptly silenced him as it whacked around the backside of his head.

"As my dull young fellow, the old sod will have his Lordship on our tails before noon, if we don't at least have a quiet word with him, and persuade him to hold his peace." Hob followed up his blow with his views on how things should proceed. "Yer a soft one Tom, but ye'll learn."

"But..." Tom interjected.

"No more buts. We are taking what we want from the old man and a bit of persuasion will keep him from raising the alarm too soon." Hob commanded. "And since ye are slow my boy to avoid doubt my persuasion will be like this." He aimed a kick at Tom which took his leg out from under him and sent him crashing into the bushes. Tom's cry of pain was quickly muffled by Bill's hand.

"Now Hob, that was uncalled for, he is a slow lad but a good un. But hush now Tom we will soon be close enough to not want to make too much of a commotion." He helped Tom back to his feet, and they carried on stealthily towards the cottage in the darkness. One of the sprites being cannier than the others hurried back to the house.

"*Lord Caledon. There are men coming to steal from Adam and do him harm.*" The thought appeared in his mind as they dared not materialise again without his say so. The returning thought was clear and concise.

"*See to it that they do not succeed. Our host and his house are under our protection and I am in the middle of some most enjoyable tales.*"

The order cascaded out to all of the nearby sprites and several of the more powerful spirits present gathered together to formulate a plan as their lord had commanded. They had free rein to prevent harm to their friend and his property. The ethereal laughter as they decided the fate of the would-be burglars would have terrified any mortal if they had been permitted to hear it.

As they neared the garden gate the three men slowed and began to move in a sporadic hunched shuffle. Tom hobbled more slowly behind the others on his sore ankle. His unwillingness growing stronger with every moment. He let the gap between him, and his companions grow bigger scanning the darkness for an opportunity to escape. A shimmering cloud of silver appeared at the edge of his vision and shot past him. It settled over the garden in front of him and it came to life with an array of icy blossoms. The beauty and delicacy of them spoke to him on a level he could not express. He sat on the ground to watch them grow and dance in the moonlight. Hob and Bill looked back as they reached the wall of the cottage and could see no sign of their young apprentice. The glamour that had engulfed his senses also concealed the boy from their sight. They exchanged a silent angry look.

"He must have taken fright. I'll tan his hide when we get back." Hob whispered. Bill nodded and indicated the door to the kitchen.

Trying the latch, it opened easily and the darkness inside gave them confidence to quickly slip across the threshold. As the door shut behind them, they waited for their eyes to adjust to the dark interior. They breathed quietly listening for clues as to where the old man was waiting.

They were temporarily blinded as a bright light exploded into being in front of them. The curses that burst from their lips echoed strangely. As their eyes adjusted they realised that they could not be in the cottage's kitchen as a colourful tiled floor spread out for what looked like miles in all directions.

They quickly span around but the door was gone. They were standing alone in a widening field of multicoloured tiles that stretched to an impossible horizon. The now gentler light was from a chandelier that hung in an empty sky and glowed of itself with no candles visible.

Bill began to run. Hob watched as each step his friend took made him sink deeper into the ground. Bill's screams only began when he realised he had now sunk up to his waist. They ended abruptly when the floor opened and gulped him down. The tiles reforming into a flat plane. Hob shivered where he stood. The panic making his eyes wide and his mouth work noiselessly.

"Ah, Hob. You will be a little harder to break I feel." A silky sounding voice whispered in his ear. He refused to look, screwing up his eyes he began to gabble out a distorted prayer. "Oh, that won't work here. You voluntarily crossed the border into our country. With such delicious hatred in your heart that the thin thread of repentance is too weak to lead you out." Hob felt the words die in his throat as he realised it was true, the prayer was a sop to his childhood fears and carried no genuine weight of belief.

"Now what shall we do with you? You don't want to run. That much is clear. Perhaps you want to put down roots?" The voice chuckled and Hob felt the presence disappear. A strange pain began in his toes, he felt them writhing and straining against his boots. He screwed his eyes tighter, until it began to feel like his legs were bursting from his trousers. Opening his eyes, he looked down and saw roots breaking free from his boots and his legs were now a single trunk that thickened and grew as he watched. His skin itched and ached as he felt the change creeping along his body as it transformed into bark. Shortly he was completely changed, and a weeping willow stood in the tiled plain. It shivered gently even though there was no breeze.

***

Adam awoke with a start. The fire had been safely banked and a blanket had been put over him as he rested in his chair. The first rays of the late winter sunrise were starting to cut through the window and wash their gentle light on the far wall.

"Good morning Adam." Lord Caledon intoned. "The tea is nearly brewed; I hope you don't mind me taking the liberty." Adam surveyed his noble fey guest and slowly waved his hand in dismissal of the thought.

"Not a jot yer lordship, a cup on waking is a treat I've not had in many a year. I am most grateful for the kindness." He accepted the proffered cup and took a sip. The natural noise of satisfaction brought a smile to the face of the fey.

"I am sorry to say that I must leave you soon, but it has been most entertaining and enlightening. For which I thank you. There was a small matter last night that nearly disrupted our conversation, but I had it taken care of." The fey sipped his own tea. "I've still to fully acquire a taste for this beverage but it does have a certain appeal."

Adam slowly levered himself out of his chair and hobbled to the window. He paused. "There seems to be a young man in my garden staring at some frost roses, sitting in the snow. Was

189

he part of the disruption?" Adam asked turning to look at the fey who continued sipping his tea.

"Oh, yes. He was. Although he was the least menacing part. You may wish to watch the next few moments, as they will be quite instructive." Lord Caledon joined Adam at the window. "His heart was not entirely bad, but we find it hard to judge you mortals, so we have put him to the test.

When the sun clears the tree line as it melts the frost roses so will it melt his heart to remove the malice. If he is mostly good he will be fine, if he is as evil as his companions were, then as it melts so will he and your garden will receive a fresh watering."

The fey eagerly watched the gradual progress of the sun. Adam's eyes fixed on the young man who seemed to be lost in a happy dream as the ice roses swayed in front of him. Adam's heart was pounding and his mouth dry, the tea forgotten in his hand. The sun's rays touched the tips of the frost flowers and they quickly melted away to nothing.

The boy slumped as they lost their sparkle and fell to the ground. Adam closed his eyes, not wishing to see the next part.

"Oh, how interesting." Lord Caledon commented, his tone so neutral that Adam was unable to decide what had occurred. Suppressing his own fears, he forced himself to look.

"He survived!" Adam shouted. Overjoyed that he hadn't unwittingly been the cause of a magical execution in his own garden.

"Apparently so. That so rarely happens. I will make a note of it. Now I must depart. Farewell Adam." the fey put down his cup, gave Adam a half bow and faded from view.

"Fare thee well, my lord. That was a night I'll not soon forget, and if nothing more there will be something to remember it by. It now looks I've a stray to look after. At my age! Ah, he can help with the lifting." Adam hobbled to his chair to retrieve his stick and went out to help the boy who had survived the Fey's magical test.

The Winter Cheer

The black carriage rattled through the large iron gates and thundered over the loose stones of the long driveway. The silver seven-pointed star in the coat of arms set in the carriage door shone brightly as it reflected back the last rays of the winter sunset. The snow on the ground glowed pink as a terrestrial echo of the beautiful sky that arched over Old Bridge Hall.

As it came to a halt outside the building the doors to the great hall creaked slowly open and Simmons, an elderly retainer, shuffled down the broad stone stairs. An eager footman bounded past him and hurried to take his position to open the carriage door to honour their guest. Once he had done so the figure that emerged from the carriage made the butler stiffen in shock.

The man who emerged was significantly taller than average with a luxurious mane of blonde hair that settled in playful and abundant waves around his broad shoulders. His richly embroidered robe shimmered and seemed to glow in the fading sunlight. His gaze drawn from the ground by the reflected splendour of the personage the footman's mouth dropped open and he gawked at their guest. The Butler's outrage at this breach of propriety overcame his own shock at the otherworldly appearance of the visitor and he resumed his formal duties.

"Greetings my lord. You must be the emissary? Your Queen's message did not divulge your name. How shall I announce you to his Lordship Viscount Old Bridge?" The years of training kept his voice from wavering and the formality of the situation brought him a sense of comfort. If he thought about this outlandish figure as just another noble guest it was easier, there were just some different oddities to politely humour.

"Must I? I suppose I must. I cannot be announced until I have been welcomed. It is a most trying paradox. The household must offer me surety of safe passage before I will grant you my name." The voice was rich and flowing. The retainer caught the gaze of the clearly still entranced footman, the narrowing of the butler's eye and a quirk of his eyebrow brought the lad back to his senses through well trained fear, and with a hasty bow the boy made his escape.

"Oh, yes. The notification of your visit made mention of that." Simmons cleared his throat. "I am empowered by his lordship St-John Algernon Perseverance Makkary, Viscount Old Bridge and his whole household. I am honoured on their behalf to offer you roof and shelter, sustenance and refreshment, free entrance and safe egress. We are all bound as your host and you agree in turn to be bound only by the obligations of the ancient rules of hospitium. This concord will abide until you have completed your task or until the 3rd sunset from this one." He spoke carefully as the formula for greeting an ambassador from the fey was not one that you wished to get wrong. The emissary stepped forward and formally grasped Simmons' forearm.

"I agree to this concord and accept your welcome. You may tell your master that Lord Caledon of the Fey, Keeper of the Third Way and Ambassador extraordinary to this mortal realm attends upon him at his earliest convenience." Simmons stepped backwards to bow and usher the guest into the building.

"Welcome Lord Caledon, Viscount Makkary apologises for not greeting you personally but he currently indisposed. His Lordship however does vouchsafe that he will attend on you at dinner, which will be in a couple of hours. If you wish I will show you to your room? We shall attend to your luggage and I will have the horses stabled. If you have any attendants I will direct them as required." Simmons continued glancing backwards to see if anyone was loitering within the darkness inside the coach.

"That is not necessary. I have everything I require here." Lord Caledon indicated a small but beautifully embroidered silken pouch at this belt. "I have brought no one to attend me and my carriage will depart until I require it once more. Our horses would not rest well in your stables anyway." The door closed without anyone touching it and the carriage began to pull away as they walked up the stairs to the doorway. "It grieves me to hear that his Lordship is unwell but I am heartened that I will see him at dinner." Simmons was touched that the lordly fey sounded genuinely concerned for the Viscount's wellbeing. Swiftly Simmons showed their guest to his room and then retreated to the safety of his other duties until it was time for dinner.

As the first reverberation of the gong died away Simmons was startled to find Lord Caledon already standing at the foot of the stair. Hiding his discomfiture, he simply bowed and guided the noble elf into the dining room. They encountered the Viscount entering from his study via another door.

"Lord Caledon, you are most welcome. An unexpected and frankly unbelievable situation, but the proofs that your Queen sent with her letter made it hard for me to either refuse her request, or discount the validity of the claims that she was sending an elf on a mission. The reason behind it remains a mystery but I hope that now you are here you can enlighten me." St-John's tone was heavy with cynicism, despite his protestations of belief. His youthful face looking older than its years, as the darkened circles under his pale eyes gave him a haunted look.

"My dear Lord Old Bridge. I will say what I can, but I believe tomorrow is the best night to discharge my mission. Let us talk of lighter things and develop our friendship. I will tell you tales of wonder if you wish, or at least appease some of your doubt that I am who I say I am." The elf's tone clearly trying to pour balm on the troubled mortal's feelings and doubts.

"Come my lord, sit. I have little appetite for tales at this time. I tried in my youth to learn the natural philosophy that so intrigued my parents but I found it impenetrable. And as for their more fanciful texts on alchemy and magic, they seemed worse than fairy tales. And yet it was to those old tomes that I turned to prepare the correct wording

196

for the formula necessary for greeting an emissary from the Fey and providing acceptable hospitality.

And if that were not enough I am now sitting to dine with that forewarned and self-proclaimed elf. I would have been in deeper doubt if your way hadn't been paved by your queen with some truly extraordinary items that I still cannot fathom. The two but twelve-sided parchment, the jug that can change any liquid into wine, and the music box that summons birds. My reason accepts that these are wonders, but they leave me baffled and lost. This is not the world that I understand." The elf watched his host closely, his blue eyes turning pale grey as he heard the sadness in St-John's voice. "Tell me of yourself. Leave the tales of wonders to those with the heart for it."

"Ah, the most wondrous of all tales is the one that you ask when seeking to avoid wonders! I am a prodigy of the Queen's court and have a fondness for the mortal realms. Born as all elves are of the heart of the magic when it strikes the earth I have been myself for nearly two hundred years and see no reason to be anyone else yet." Lord Caledon smiled but failed to elicit any response from his host. Simmons entered quietly carrying two small bowls of soup.

"Two hundred? Yet you don't look much older than I. And I've yet to reach thirty." St-John took his spoon and absentmindedly began to eat his soup.

"We can look how we wish." Lord Caledon replied. "Observe." He then proceeded to change his features subtly at first and then in increasingly bizarre ways. Altering his hair and skin through various modes at points mimicking beasts of the earth and air. St-John observed, unphased. Taking mouthful after mouthful of soup. A little surprised his display had not moved his host more strongly Lord Caledon resignedly began to eat his soup, or at least tried.

"Is there perhaps some pepper and salt?" Lord Caledon enquired scanning the table for any sign of seasoning.

"Oh, somewhere no doubt. Simmons. See to it." St-John requested putting down his own spoon, having emptied the bowl. Simmons quickly fetched the requested seasonings from a side press, with murmured apologies for the oversight. Lord Caledon added much and then quickly consumed the still barely palatable soup.

The remainder of the meal progressed in the same manner, each course bland at best and the conversation of a similar quality. The fey hid his gratitude when his host announced it was his plan to retire soon after they had consumed the final course. The struggle the mortal was barely winning to sustain even the simplest courtesy was plain to the elf. But rather than taking offence as so many of his kind would have done at the perceived disrespect, he delved deeper. As he felt the shape of his host's soul he could sense no malice, just a deep grey sadness which enveloped the Viscount.

Beginning to return to his room he paused, he felt someone calling to him. Walking down the dim corridor Lord Caledon opened his senses to the house and followed his instincts. They led him to knock on the door three further down from his own grand bedroom.

"Come in." an elderly voice called to him and he entered. "Ye'll be the elf then." the same voice continued, Lord Caledon's eyes were already adjusting to the low light, by glowing a warm golden colour. "Come in, come in and shut the door behind ye, I can't bear the draught. And step into the light as I would see ye more closely. I hear that ye are a handsome devil." He quickly spotted the source of the summons. Buried in a bundle of blankets by the fire in a large bath chair sat a small and very old woman.

"I thank you for the invitation. You flatter me, but then we do so love flattery." Lord Caledon took a seat opposite her. The soft light of the flames dancing on his fine features. "To whom do I have the pleasure of speaking?"

"I'm Maggie. A relict that hasn't quite yet mouldered away, but I think tis my last winter if these aches in my bones have anything to say about it." She sounded surprisingly upbeat despite the casual dismissal in her words of the likelihood of her imminent death. "I was a maid to St-John's grandmother and the last one in the household who knew his parents well. Tis why he keeps me close. Poor soul." The last words dropped almost to a whisper.

"Ah, the infamous Maggie Wood? I heard tell of you many years ago. Still this side of the veil indeed. Allow me?" Lord Caledon reached over and gently took one of her thin and veiny hands. A golden glow flowed from him and spread into her until a gentle shimmer had passed over her whole body.

"Oh, that was wonderful." She straightened in her chair. "Oh! That was wonderful indeed. I thank ye most kindly my Lord. That was a true kindness." The happiness in her voice made her sound more youthful.

"It was a small thing. Just a bit of balm from one old soul to another." Lord Caledon withdrew his hand and stared into the fire. "I do have a favour to ask in return however, tell me, how is it that St-John has become so lost?" The idle tone matched his posture, but Maggie's shrewd eyes detected more than he was trying to reveal.

"Ah, that's it. Butter me up and see what I spill!" She clutched the blankets around her like a shield. Lord Caledon slowly turned his golden eyes to meet hers, and as she saw them fade to reveal an inner grey sadness she felt her resistance falter.

"It is important to my mission that I know what sort of man he is." Lord Caledon stated and returned to looking into the flames which danced in the mirror of his eyes. Maggie sat and watched him for a few moments pondering her words.

"He is a good one, and young still, but the losses he has had broke him this last year. Ye'd think orphaned so young he'd be tougher, but he kept his heart soft. Sadly, his head remained so too! He means well I know but for the son of one of the sharpest men, and that wife of his was smarter by far, their son turned out good hearted but unwise.

The old Viscount, gods rest him, trained his heir, but didn't raise him as a boy who would be a man, just a set of duties but with no heart. Twas

Adam who kept him right mostly, gave him the human side of things. After he was so close to Alfie back in his youth. So Adam over time became like a second father; he was close to the boy, when he could be." Maggie wiped a small tear away.

"Anyway, when Adam passed in the spring just gone it was like St-John had sprung a leak. He's been slowly draining away ever since." Maggie turned and stared into the fire too. The weight of the memories easier to bear after the elf's magic had taken some of the pain away, but they still struck deep.

"So, it is simple grief and loss? He still has a good heart?" Lord Caledon turned his eyes onto the elderly maid, seeking her assessment. Feeling his gaze she nodded.

"Aye. If he finds joy again he will be right as rain, but it has so far been a hard road and without his compass he is lost." She kept staring into the fire, becoming lost in her own thoughts. She heard her guest rise and head to the door.

"Sleep well Maggie. Until tomorrow." Shutting the door behind himself he left her alone with her memories.

***

The next morning, the day was bright and frosty. Lord Caledon ventured out to walk the grounds and speak to some of the local spirits and sprites. "Bright Solstice" being the greeting of choice they exchanged on that day and they exchanged small tokens of goodwill. With a plan taking shape in his mind some small requests were made by the Lordly fey that his people were only too happy to oblige. This task completed Lord Caledon returned indoors and spent the day in the library absorbing the atmosphere redolent with the memories of people who were no more.

As sunset approached he knew it was time. He strode into the hallway and with a wave of his hand made the gong reverberate so loudly and for so long that the whole household hurried to work out the cause of the commotion. Even frail Maggie Wood was at the top step peering down short-sightedly from her bath chair. Eventually St-John Makkary emerged from his study looking even more haggard and angry at the disruption.

"My Lord Caledon! What is the meaning of this?" St-John bellowed over the still vibrating gong, which was silenced just as suddenly by another wave of the elvish lord's hand.

"My apologies Lord Old Bridge. It was a necessary element to my mission. Before the sun has set on this shortest day I must vouchsafe to thee and thy household the purpose of my mission! Many years past a boon was promised which was never claimed, until recently. And the delivery of that promise was delayed by circumstances beyond my control, but now by order of her majesty Queen Mab of the Highest Court of the Fey, I, Lord Caledon as her Ambassador extraordinary and the Keeper of the Third Way do hereby present to thee, Lord St-John Makkary, Viscount Old Bridge and to thy descendants until the end of mortal realms, this gift." Reaching into his belt pouch his hand and forearm disappeared more deeply than it seemed possible until it emerged once more holding a bough of mistletoe. The green of the leaves looked vibrant and the berries were pearly white, in the last rays of sunset it shimmered with a faint golden aura.

"This bough of mistletoe I gift thee as a symbol of the cheer that comes in the darkest times. When hearts are lifted in good company, even the longest night can be safely navigated and the bright dawn that follows will be for everyone the balm that they need to heal. All souls will be renewed as the seasons and as the sun." Lord Caledon strode towards the now shocked looking Viscount. The household were all standing watching awed at the spectacle unfolding before them. Placing the bough of mistletoe in his host's unresisting hand the elf stood back and bowed deeply.

"I… I… Thank you most kindly, and your Queen." St-John stammered out his response. The mistletoe's shimmer spread into him as he held it. The weariness faded from his eyes. "Heavens, you are right,. It is the solstice! We must have a feast. Everyone! Help me! We need decorations, and food!" St-John appealed to his staff and as he moved around the hall the contagious mood of excitement spread through everyone. They had resigned themselves to a simple meal and an early night, as all the other nights had been this winter. But their confusion was replaced by spreading joy as the elf's promise and the Viscount's response kindled hope and the prospect of merriment.

Lord Caledon joined in the preparations and with the aid of his magical pouch was able to contribute to both the decorations and the food. He hurried around the place up and down the hall with St-John and the household making the place feel festive. The laughter and kindness that the household were sharing and showing to each other making more difference than a combination of all of the other preparations.

As the feast was being set on the table, and St-John's instruction was that everyone was to join him in the main hall, there came an unexpected knocking on the door. St-John in his exuberance went and opened the door himself to find a large man bundled in his black cloak supporting a young woman in a rich purple cloak. The evening outside had unnoticed within the hall turned wild and he quickly beckoned them in out of the rising winds.

"Fetch your master! We need shelter and assistance. My daughter took quite a tumble when our carriage wheel broke!" The large man tersely instructed St-John and was most affronted when his orders were met with loud laughter, both from St-John and some passing servants.

"My apologies sir, but you have caught us quite at a moment of disruption. If you will pardon me the breach of protocol, but I am the master of this house. Allow me to introduce myself, I am St-John Makkary and I welcome you Sir and your daughter to my home. Simmons! Fetch some assistance for the lady!" He smiled and offered his hand. The man turned pale at the offence he felt he must have caused and began to stammer out his profuse apologies. They quickly got his daughter settled into a chair and warm glasses of wine were provided to them both.

"I am Sir Reginald Anker, and this is my daughter Persephone." the man introduced himself once they had calmed him down. "Our carriage skidded on some ice by your gate and the wheel broke. Our coach man is freeing the horses, but we had to seek shelter."

"Simmons! Send someone to help Sir Reginald's coachman please!" St-John directed his attentive assistant.

"At once My Lord." the elderly retainer responded and hurried off.

"You are most welcome to join us for the solstice feast; it is just now being served. All are welcome." St-John offered.

"That is most kind my Lord." Persephone answered before her father could offer any other response. She smiled at St-John and offered him her hand to help her up. As they stood the first strains of music could be heard from the dining hall. "Oh, this is magical!" St-John smiled and began to walk towards the door. Seeing Lord Caledon standing to one side, he apologised and directed his new guests to proceed without him. Their wonder drew them on unprotesting into the dining hall.

"Will you not join us?" St-John begged the elf. "This is all your doing and we must drink your health and you must eat your share of the feast!"

207

"My mission is ended, and so by our concord I could now depart. But I will stay at your request. Is that your wish?" the elf's eyes were now deep green and glittering with flecks of warm gold.

"You are my guest and I will not hear of you leaving so soon. The concord gave you until the third sunset and it would be most inhospitable of me to cast you out before dinner. Anyway my dear guest I believe that you have some tales to tell, and I have found anew my appetite for wonder!" St-John took the Fey's elbow and guided him into the hall where the whole household and their guests were sharing merriment and would scare away the darkest night through celebration and companionship. The sounds of laughter and music reached out to the woods where the local spirits danced in the snow and made their own celebration to speed the new dawn. The solstice turns and darkness gives way to light, and so the years span on in that merry dance.

***

The steady tap, tap, tap of the stick echoed through the wooden halls. The deep silence of winter had settled on the land, on the hall, and on the hearts of those who lived there. The bright

208

sunshine illuminating the room did nothing to lift the spirit of Archibald Makkary, Viscount Old Bridge. The war might have been over, but the cost was still being paid. His dog padded alongside and looked up at his master seeking attention which was sadly lacking. Letting himself into the library Archibald found the family gathered in gloomy companionable solitude. Under the kindly gazes of his ancestors St-John and Persephone Makkary, looking down from the canvas above the fireplace. Each of the current crop of Makkarys present sat at their own endeavour but used the proximity of others to lessen the dull ache of sadness that filled them all.

"Good Morning family." Archibald said as he lowered himself into his habitual seat in the big leather chair by the fire, picking up the neatly folded newspaper he settled in to join them in their communal reverie.

"Good Morning dear." his wife Agnes responded; her hands still occupied with the needlepoint that seemed to be her constant work. The half glasses perched on her nose helping her see the delicate stitches that she was making. His son and daughter in-law issued faint murmurs of response but did not further stir themselves from their own distractions.

The idle ticking of the clock and the crackle of the fire were the regular sounds that filled the room, only interrupted by the rustling of paper or the snip of scissors. The dull silence reigned until the door creaked open once again and a new figure burst into the room in a flurry of activity.

"Is there any tea? I'm parched and frozen all together and that is most dreary." the youngest member of Makkary household entered. Her bright tone at odds with the ponderous solemnity that filled the room.

"Sybil dear, that is not the way a lady announces her presence. We missed you at breakfast. It is more polite to enquire after our health than to be so blunt and to seek refreshment." She eyed her daughter pointedly over her glasses and sighed when she saw that her reproach was falling on deaf ears. "Very well, it is a suitable time. Please ring the bell." Sybil had barely waited for her mother to finish the sentence before she had reached for the bell pull and given it an eager tug. Lady Makkary instructed the butler to fetch the tea when he materialised, and she carefully tidied away her needlework.

"Sorry Mother. It was so gloriously bright this morning I wanted to go for a walk while the snow was still crisp and unbroken. But there is another fall just starting so there will be several more inches before long. It is so beautiful. But it is dreadfully chilly out there. I will need to dig out some warmer things." She settled herself on the low padded fender by the fire and extended her hands towards the flames.

"Sybil, really. You must stop these excursions, especially when you haven't told anyone. There was a certain amount of licence before, but now we are getting back to normality, it really must stop." Her mother leant forward to take her daughter's hands "Look at me. Can't you see that this wilfulness is most unbecoming?" Agnes found herself suddenly speechless when her daughter turned to face her. The steely determination that was in her daughter's eyes left no doubt that this was not going to go her way.

"Yes Mother. I am aware that it is unbecoming, and along with the hundreds of other injunctions that I keep myself pretty, quiet and heaven's know what else. However as much as I love you I am most unwilling to allow something like 'what other people think' change how I wish to live. This place has become a mausoleum and I am not going to fade away or just be as quiet as these portraits. Anyway, since the war is over now…" Sybil stayed seated, but her voice filled the room.

"Hush now." Her sister-in-law suddenly interjected. "You know we don't talk about it." The room fell silent as the butler entered with the tea things. The general rattling of china and spoons gave the illusion of peace while the shockwaves of Sybil's free-spirited behaviour rippled through the family group's minds. Once the butler left the spell was broken again.

"This is the 20th Century for heaven's sake Elizabeth. I don't see why I can't be myself and the war was only a smidgen of why I think things need to change." The family stoically ignored her appeal to modernity. "I miss him desperately, but we can't all just pretend that we are dead too. Stephen died, not us! And George. You are almost as bad, since you came back it is like you didn't! It is all very unfair!" Sybil's use of the name which none of them had dared speak in the months since the telegram deepened the chill in the air rather than moving them to agree that they were still alive.

"Sybil. That is enough. You are upsetting your mother, and you shouldn't take that tone. You know it hasn't been easy on any of us." Archibald interjected from his seat by the fireplace.

"But Father, it really isn't fair. George, you agree don't you?" She turned to her brother, his face carefully still as he sipped his tea.

"Sorry Sibs, but you are making a scene."
He guiltily glanced at the other family members
and tried to make it sound apologetic.

"Oh, fine. If that's how it is. I will go for
another walk!" Sybil stormed from the room; the
family continued to drink their tea in strained
silence, the ticking clock keeping them company.

Sybil grabbed her coat from where she had
left it by the door and headed out into the gently
falling snow. The crisp crunch of her swift progress
the only sound in the magical world created by the
snow swirling around her. The heat of her anger
made her breath billow in the chill air more wildly
and explosively around her. As she approached the
woods her initial energetic outburst diminished.
The simple vastness of the cold and silence outside
leeching her body into a gentle numbness while
inside her heart the fire still burned at a white heat.

Pausing at the forest's edge she stood and
watched her breath filling the air around her with
transient vapours. "I am a Dragon!" She shouted
and then giggled at the thought.

"Oh, is that what you are? I thought you
were a human. My apologies for my foolish
misapprehension most noble Wyrm." Sybil started
at this unexpected response.

"Who's there?" She looked around. "Is that you John? Don't be a silly boy. I'll tell cook that you were misbehaving again." Sybil felt panic rising, even as she spoke, she knew that it was not John's voice. This was that of a grown man, a stranger, not the gardener's boy. And even in those few words it held a powerful resonance that made her feel deeply uncomfortable.

"I am not John. But I know who you are. Sybil Makkary." The figure stepped from behind a tree at the edge of the wood. He was tall and wearing an old-fashioned looking cloak. The hood was down and the smiling face, framed by waves of blond hair, was beautiful in a way that Sybil had never seen before.

"You look like one of Botticelli's angels! Oh. My apologies that was so rude of me. And I'm sorry that you heard me being so silly, about being a dragon and all that. It is just how I felt. So hot and bothered inside and only able to make the world see it through making steam. Please ignore that it was just silliness." Sybil blushed with embarrassment at the thought of looking foolish. "Are you here to see Father? Or George? I didn't know we were expecting anyone. I thought this Christmas was going to be dull, and so sad. Even with the war over. What with Stephen being gone

214

and George still so sad after it all. It just isn't fair. I'm terribly sorry I am just wittering on. What's your name?" She paused and observed the face of the stranger, he smiled broadly as she allowed her words to tumble out.

"I am in fact here to see you Sybil. I was passing by and felt the need to give you a message. Walk with me a short while." Sybil nodded, the stranger's manner was oddly reassuring, and his eyes were a kind deep brown with flecks of green. The green in them reminded her of dear departed Stephen's eyes. They fell into step alongside each other, the crunch of the fresh snow underfoot counterpointing the gentle flow of their conversation.

"It is not right that Yule, or Christmas as you call it, should be dull. The days are dark, but that is when people's hearts should be merry to bide through the darkness. I hear your pain, and how you try to hide it through this silliness, but I also feel the pain of the others in your household. Your family have been here a long time and that counts for something in my eyes, it provides some continuity which is otherwise lacking and you can share your joy more easily with others.

The losses so many have experienced have drained the joy from your world. However when the world itself is scarce of that joy we must strive harder to stir it back to life. I hear now that for you all the silent echo of sadness is deafening, and it drowns out all other sounds. But gentle Sybil I am here to tell you that with a good will there are other strains of music that can be played to bring forth joy that will end that silence.

The healing of hearts is no easy matter, but after such a harrowing it means that the soil of the soul can take the seed of joy more easily. If it is replanted and nurtured it can grow again and it must to prevent your heart becoming cold and barren. And in you, sweet child, there is a delicate sprout of hope, but it must be watered.

My message to you is simple. Return to your family and seek out the seeds of happiness that have been garnered away for safe keeping. They will help you all find your new joy rather than let your hearts wither through the frostbite of mourning for that which has faded. Mortals are fleeting, but therefore your happiness is all the more precious for that fact." The wind picked up and a sudden flurry of snow stung her eyes and made her blink.

"That is most kind, I don't understand it, but how can I find seeds of joy?" She turned to look and the stranger was gone. She was alone in the middle of an open section of the gardens. Looking down she saw that hers were the only footprints in the snow. She ran back to the house her heart pounding. She closed the door and leant against it, panting heavily as she wondered what had just happened to her.

"Sibby? Are you okay old chum? You look like you've seen a ghost." George shuffled towards her, his voice neutral and as lacking in emphasis as it had been since he returned home after his service concluded. Sybil began to giggle hysterically at his comment and rushed to hug him. He was taken aback by her sudden demonstration of emotion but hugged her and felt her calm down quickly in his arms.

"Oh Gee-gee. Do you remember how it used to be when we were kids? You and Phen used to tease me so much, but we were happy weren't we? And Christmas. It is nearly here, remember how much Phen loves, no sorry, loved Christmas?" Sybil stepped back from her brother. "And so, did you. I know it has been tough, but George, Gee-gee. It is over. The worst of it anyway. Father and Mother just sort of shut down over it all and it was like they wanted time to stop. If we didn't move forward then maybe it wasn't the case that he wasn't coming back. That it would stop the time that he was here from getting further away. But I don't think that this will help any of us remember how to smile again." Sybil wiped the tears from her face. The sadness in her eyes making her seem like the little girl that she had been when they were little Phen, Gee-gee and Sibs.

"Come on old girl. I've got an idea. Buck up!" He grabbed her hand and slowly began the walk up the stairs, ignoring her complaints and queries until they reached the small door that he remembered.

"Isn't that the attic?" Sybil asked still deeply confused, but feeling hopeful and trusting that George had an idea.

"It is Sibs, and that is where we will find Christmas!" His voice cracked as he said that, the emotional dam that had been keeping him safe from his own feelings began to leak. "Up we go." He led her up the narrow stairs, the dim light above them showing just enough to guide them upwards. When they reach the dusty attic, they split up and began to look around the boxes and chests that were scattered around the place.

Sybil felt her eyes drawn to one particular chest. It seemed to her that there a glow coming from within it. It was subtle but it seemed to be creeping out through the crack of the lid and making the keyhole glow like a tiny ember. Opening the lid, the treasures inside were what she was looking for. Heaps of tinsel and dried winter flower garlands, and in the centre was a bough of mistletoe. It still looked fresh, the berries a bright pearl white despite being locked away in a chest for a long time. She picked it up and triumphantly waved it in the air.

"Gee-Gee! I've found Christmas!" She quickly gathered some of the tinsel and wrapped it around her neck. She began to giggle, and her brother laughed at the sight of his sister, waving mistletoe and wearing her tinsel boa. The last vestiges of winter sunshine were washing through the dusty windows and making it look as if she was glowing in her borrowed festive finery.

"Sibs! You have indeed. Let's see if we can get some of this downstairs and help Mother and Father remember as well." He joined her at the chest and picked out some of the other decorations. "You were right, it hasn't been fair, but we can only make things better by trying."

Sybil hugged her brother again before they went back down the stairs.

"Maybe we can help them to see that it is possible to be happy even when you have lost so much. As the memories are still there and they don't get stronger by being locked away. And who knows maybe we can plant some new memories? We are still here, and you are right. We have to keep on trying. Welcome back Gee-Gee. I, so very much, missed you."

Heading back downstairs they launched into a medley of Christmas carols that had the rest of the household initially wondering if they were drunk, but then slowly they all began to join in. The ability to resist joining in on a good 'fa-la-la-la-la' was beyond even the heaviest heart. The music kept spreading through the household one voice at a time and brightening the early evening as they turned on the lights. After some initial doubts they eventually cajoled their father and mother into letting them decorate the hall for Christmas.

The mistletoe and the other decorations an outward sign of the remembered joy that they could all still share, especially at a time of darkness.

"I think you are right Sibs. We only get a brighter tomorrow if you keep moving towards it. Thank you for helping me remember." George handed his sister another glass of mulled wine and they smiled at the noisy gathering of the family and staff. The previous strained silence now being drowned out by merry singing.

The Peace Bringer

The door clicked shut behind him. The sound of a heavy suitcase hitting the laminate floor echoed briefly off the plain white walls. He revelled in the simple silence of home. After the hectic commute through a winter nightmare of canned Christmas music, icy roads, and panicked people buying random presents, it was beautiful to just stand for a moment and breathe.

"I'm home!" Adam shouted into the quiet flat. "Hello?" He tilted his head, listening for a response. When none came he began flicking through the pile of post on the small table in the hallway. Most of them were circulars addressed to the occupier, and there were one or two bills. Partially concealed in the folds of sheaf of cheap advertising leaflets was one unusual envelope.

It was addressed to both of them, 'Mr I Makkary & Mr A Wynne'. It was a neatly printed label with impressive calligraphy and was framed by a small banner of silver glitter. It was definitely thicker than a Christmas card. The stationery was heavy and textured, he had a sinking feeling.

Flipping it over he saw the return address and felt the final slump in his mood as it confirmed what he suspected. It was from Iain's family.

221

Tapping it against his hand he made his way into the living room. That was where he found Iain, fast asleep.

He was sprawled on the sofa with his headphones on, amidst the debris of food wrappers and discarded jackets and shoes. His tousled black hair making him look younger than his years. In sleep his face looked more innocent, it was because you couldn't see the wicked glint that was a near permanent fixture in his eyes.

Adam stood and just enjoyed the sight of his slumbering boyfriend, even the mess didn't bother him, that much. Crossing the room, he gently touched Iain's shoulder to wake him. Iain's brief disorientation at being woken up was quickly replaced by a warm smile.

"Welcome home lover!" Iain said pulling Adam in for a kiss. His hand smoothing over Adam's close cropped and thinning blonde hair. "You've had a trim." He smiled as he gently rubbed his hand over the soft stubble. "I like it like this." Adam lowered himself onto the couch and settled his head on Iain's lap.

"And I like when you do that." He purred happily. "I've missed you. I am so happy that I'm able to be here with you for Christmas. Quality time with my family. Oh. I nearly forgot. We got this." He waved the envelope under Iain's nose and let him take it and look at it closely.

He briefly looked confused at the unusual envelope until he too turned it over and read the return address. The heavy sigh of frustration resonated down into his body and Adam felt it in Iain's stomach by his ear. Iain threw the envelope onto the floor without opening it.

"Hey. Don't do that, we'll never find it again." Adam chuckled at his own joke; his laughter ended abruptly as Iain rose to his feet dislodging him.

"Oh! And what do you mean by that? Yeah I know it's a mess, but I'm not the fucking maid! You're barely ever here, so don't give me grief about the place not being spick and span. If it bothers you that much get a cleaner." Iain stood in the middle of the room shouting. Adam couldn't keep the shock from his face at the abrupt change and watched as Iain turned and fled the room.

"Iain! Honey! I'm sorry, it was just a joke." Adam stayed on the couch and called after him but got no response. He sighed heavily and slumped back into the cushions. He decided to leave it for a few minutes, the initial flare up of Iain's temper was always the worst bit.

He also needed a couple of minutes to unwind and make sure he didn't make any more ill-timed jokes. The travel had been long, running through multiple time zones always left him feeling a bit grumpy. He stifled a yawn.

"Lunchtime is not bedtime." He muttered to himself. Prying himself from the sofa to avoid the risk of an ill-timed nap he began to tidy up the immediate mess. Picking up the discarded letter he propped it on the coffee table.

Taking the empty food wrappers into the kitchen he was bundling them up to put them in the bin when a name on the delivery slip jumped out at him. 'Raphael' was scrawled at the top of the receipt.

"Raphael! You had Raphael here?!" Adam shouted and stalked back out of the kitchen the crumpled bag in his hand and was halfway across the floor when Iain appeared at the bedroom door. His face half in shadow from the slanting angle of the low winter sunlight, he could still make out the chagrined grimace that was twisting Iain's face. "How could you?!" Adam felt the hot tears begin to form in his eyes.

"It was only dinner. I was going to tell you. He is sober now. He came to say sorry; to make amends, he is working through those steps. You know about making up for his mistakes." Iain's own anger had evaporated and been replaced with guilt so he tried to calm Adam who was clearly struggling to not shout.

"Mistakes! He spiked your drink and nearly killed you. With that fucking cocktail he mixed up with god knows what shit he was on in it. I'm never going to forgive him for that. Never! I don't understand how you can be so fucking calm!" Adam wiped away his tears and threw the crumpled paper bag on the floor. Settling himself in an armchair he rested his head in his shaking hands and began to deliberately slow his breathing.

"I know. I nearly didn't see him, but Theresa called me first. And she pleaded his case first really well. She said that I should at least listen to his apology. She came too and was here the whole time. I'm sorry. I should have told you, I was going to, after you were home. But I wanted to hear him out first. I knew you would have told me not to let him in." Iain knelt by his boyfriend and took one of his trembling hands giving it a gentle squeeze.

"I nearly lost you. That night was the worst of my whole life. And that bastard was the reason." Adam slowly raised his head and pulled Iain towards him kissing his head and holding him close in an awkward seated embrace.

"I know. It seems odd I barely remember it. For me it went from being at the party, to nothing, to feeling like shit in a hospital bed for a day or so. It was only afterwards that I realised how messed up it all was." Iain murmured into this lover's shoulder. They stayed like that for a few more minutes. Iain moved himself backwards on his heels so that he could crouch down still holding on to Adam's hands. He made eye contact and then smiled. They both wiped the tears from their eyes and after a quick nod they hugged again.

"Shall we find out what the family are summoning us to?" Iain asked gesturing across to the envelope. Adam nodded still gulping back the last residue of the anger and fear that had suddenly swept through him. Iain settled himself on the edge of sofa and casually ripped open the envelope. Separating the card from a folded bundle of paper his eyes quickly scanned over it.

"Bloody hell!" He muttered and handed the card over to Adam. Adam's curiosity getting the better of him he moved over to sit next to Iain as he read it.

"So, she did it then! The lesbians have beaten us to it. Arabella is marrying Susan! And in the family church as well!" Adam grinned as he read the invitation.

"Mother will be livid!" Iain exclaimed. "Auntie Emma has gone all out on this it seems. Look at that gilt writing. You could concuss someone with this! I should have known that something was afoot. Auntie Em was all over me in July and making pointed comments about blood being thicker than water. Mother was fuming, after Auntie Em had been the one to make some of the snide comments when I came out about it not being a shock!"

Adam picked up the sheaf of papers and began browsing through the nearly encyclopaedic instructions and details about how Susan and Arabella's 'special day' was going to unfold in a series of apparently carefully choreographed, and probably very costly, events.

"So will we be going then?" Adam enquired. "I've always wondered how the rest of your family got on. And it's been what, only nine years since we got together and last Christmas was the first time I met them?" He smiled to take the sting out of the comment, but the teasing didn't flow quite as easily. Iain looked tense again.

"Oh. Yeah. It will be quite the social event. I suppose it will be easier, all the homosexuals will be coming out of the woodwork that day, so we might as well take advantage of that coverage, heck even Uncle Gus won't be able to be too overtly homophobic, if he dares to show up. It seems that the lesbians have led the way." Iain picked up the pile of instruction papers and began reading through the detailed account of the anticipated big day. "Bloody hell, all that's missing is a circus!" He muttered.

"No, check page 4." Adam responded. Iain's mouth dropped open and he began to furiously read through the remaining pages. "Sorry. No. I'm teasing! Although it is a close-run thing." Adam chuckled at the way Iain twisted his mouth into a rueful grin.

"You evil git. You know I wouldn't have put it passed them. But yeah. I think we have to go. They have been slowly coming around to the fact that their 'son and heir' isn't marrying a local debutant. At least they weren't able to blame you for corrupting me, the honour of that misplaced accusation fell to Peter at University. They hated him, even if he was just the scapegoat so they didn't have to accept that I was just naturally gay. That was followed by a few years of tense phone calls and chilly texts. They actually occasionally ask me about how you are doing. And that, if nothing else, proves they are thawing slowly to me, or to us Also they did give me that box of stuff from the clear out of the old house." Iain threw the final pages back onto the coffee table. "Are we okay?" He turned in his seat. Adam had withdrawn again a little, the distraction provided by the invitation had been short lived.

"Yeah, it was just a shock. I hate him so much and thinking that you might have been at risk again just set me off." Adam felt his fists clenching at the resurging memory. Iain rested his hand on Adam's arm, his eyes searching his lover's face. Seeking to re-establish their connection.

"I'm sorry that I did it without telling you, and that is how you found out. I'm glad that we have discussed it now. I would have hated keeping it from you any longer, but I just didn't think a text would cut it and I couldn't face doing that on a call either, international arguments are the worst.

Anyway. In other news we have Richard and Oscar coming around tomorrow for dinner. So it is best that we did this now. They would have loved to see this scene. They're still talking to Ra... him on occasion you know. They might have brought it up just to rile you." Iain kept this tone matter of fact.

"Oh yes. I love them both dearly, but they do love a bit of drama. And aren't above making it when it's in short supply." Adam looked around the living room. "If they are coming tomorrow we need to get this place sorted then!"

"What do you mean? It won't take us that long to tidy up." Iain asked reaching down to pick up his jacket.

"The only sign of Christmas are those cards next to the telly. I think we need to up our game! Tell you what. I'll go and find a tree if you dig out the decorations. If I get within 5 feet of that bed I reckon I will end up asleep and that will ruin my plan to ride this jet-lag out." He got to his feet and headed to the door. "The fresh air will do me good and help me clear my head."

Iain watched him go. Sighing a little when he heard the door slam he levered himself off the sofa and went to dig through the boxes and see if he could find their decorations.

In the cupboard on top of the other boxes he found the small suitcase that his Mother had given him, a random selection of things that had been distributed to the family following the clear out of the old house. A random selection of dusty mementos and heirlooms that were possibly worthless, but you never knew.

Coming from an old family sometimes odd things got passed down. Along with a selection of old letters and a very battered teddy bear whose name escaped him, was a small flat fabric wrapped bundle. The embroidery on it frayed and faded, but it seemed to have been very special to someone. Curious he sat on the floor and laid it out so that he could begin to unfold it. The layers opened easily releasing a mixed smell of mustiness and a strange spicy aroma that he couldn't place. The final layers folded away to reveal a bough of mistletoe. It looked fresh, despite the years, his first guess was that it was probably just high-quality plastic.

Carefully picking it up he was surprised to discover it was real. He shook his head when his eyes deceived him as he thought it shimmered gold briefly. Looking up he wondered what angle the car headlights must have been at to reflect so oddly. The leaves still felt springy, and the berries looked white and moist.

"Perfect, that is the start of the decorations at least." He muttered and put the mistletoe to one side, putting everything else back in the suitcase. He went back into the cupboard to hunt out the main decorations. Finding the box quite quickly he lugged it into the living room. Pausing for a moment he rummaged through the Christmas box and took out a strip of golden ribbon. Collecting the mistletoe from the bedroom he found the perfect spot from the light fitting at the entrance to the living area and hung the mistletoe. Going to his laptop he picked a random online festive playlist to try and help him get into the right mood. The strains of Christmas music filled the flat as he carried on sorting through his boxes and making other preparations.

When Adam returned triumphant he sounded much happier. "Is that Mulled Wine I smell?" He asked as he dragged the small mesh wrapped pine tree into the living room.

"Yes. It is! I might be easily influenced by the music but I decided that we should have wine to go with the mistletoe!" He pointed at the bough hanging behind Adam.

"Lovely. Come on, give me a hand. It's only a small tree, but bugger is it heavy when you have to lug it a couple of miles." Iain hurried over and joined Adam in getting the tree to the right part of the room. They screwed the base into the wood to make it stable, once it was up they cut the mesh containing the branches. As they unfurled a small shower of needles scattered onto the carpet.

"Lovely. It smells great. Thank you for getting it! I love a real tree." Iain smiled and disappeared into the kitchen returning with two steaming mugs of mulled wine.

"And thank you. That also smells great." Adam sipped the alcoholic brew and breathed a contented sigh. "Perfect. It is freezing out there. Just what I needed."

They settled onto the sofa and took a few minutes to just sip their wine and look at the tree.

"Ready?" Adam asked.
"Ready." Iain responded.

They sat down on the floor in front of the tree and together they opened the main box that contained their decorations. They began to remove little boxes and wrapped packages that they set out in rows between them in preparation for the ritual that they had evolved over the past few years.

Flashing Adam a nervous smile Iain reached out and picked up one of the parcels and unwrapped it. Slowly peeling away the layers of paper the hidden treasure inside was revealed. A small plastic bier stein. The words "Fröhliche Weihnachten von Bayern" were just about visible on the side and were flaking a little.

"Ah, Munich!" Iain dangled the little ornament between his fingers. "What? Seven years ago?" Iain pondered

"Yes, seven." Adam responded.

"Ah yes. We stayed at that hotel tucked away on that residential street. It was that long weekend we took, to go and see the Christmas market. God everything was so overpriced, but the lights were stunning. We picked this up on the second night. You were trying to get change for something and we both agreed it was hideous, so we had to buy it. I remember seeing the first flakes of snow falling as we walked along, the streets were so busy and you kept on looking at the people and the crowd, but I just wanted to look at the lights and so I saw it coming and I made you stop."

"You did, I was so irritated that night, I couldn't work out why you kept on drifting along aimlessly. The crowd was insane, and I thought you were going to be bounced off into the scrum without me noticing. You took my hand and pulled me to one side. We found that little nook by the edge of a shop, by the Victualienmarkt and you made me stop and actually look at what was happening. The flakes were so small to start with, and silent, but the way that they danced down. It was just beautiful. Thank you."

Adam leant forward and kissed him before Iain stood and put the first decoration on the tree. Now it was his turn.

He slowly drifted his hand over the selection of packages and picked one, wrapped in red paper. He chuckled when he had peeled off the wrapping and dangled the prize for Iain to see.

"The Crapper! Barcelona, four years ago." Adam smiled. "Jordi!" His giggle became naughty at the memory.

"Oh, Jordi. That boy had no shame!" Iain joined in the laughter.

"We were back from Sitges and taking a day or so to see the sights of the city. Landmarks rather than the wildlife on the beach. And we were staying in that tiny Air BnB place somewhere along that ridiculously long street."

"Avinguda Diagonal" Iain interjected taking a sip of his mulled wine.

"That was it, putting Diagon Alley to shame you said! Not that you are a size queen!" Adam continued while Iain pouted at him comically. "We were escaping from La Rambla. I don't know why you drag me into those crowds.

Any way we found this cute little bar that was barely a hole in the wall where we stop for a mojito or two. And you then start flirting outrageously with the pretty young barfly at the next table."

"Oi. You told me to as well. He was giving us both the eye and you thought it would be fun!" Iain interrupted.

"That is true. And was I wrong?" Adam smiled and they both laughed.

"So as we both know, one thing lead to another and next thing we know it's midnight and Jordi is leading us both upstairs, a hand down each of our shorts. We thought he was shouting for his German flatmate called Claus to let him in and only then worked out that he was trying to tell us to get his keys out. We had picked up some Spanish, but the Catalan threw us a little." They both collapsed in laughter.

"The poor boy had run out of hands. What was he to do?!" Iain managed to gasp out through his giggles.

"Very true. And that was a lot of fun." Adam continued sipping his own wine. "And then the next morning we ended up having to follow him to work. We were so very lost and far too hungover to work out where we were going. And he was working on the stall for his sister in law and he got so embarrassed when we arrived with him that we pretended it was all just a coincidence. I foolishly agreed to buy some things from her to disguise the situation.

I don't think your Mother ever quite got over her porcelain version of this little fellow. And now to remember our wild night we have this little crapper. I propose a toast to the heath of Jordi and El Caganer." Iain echoed the toast and they both drank. Adam stood up and hung the decoration on the tree.

"She never really accepted my 'but it's cultural' argument." Iain said as he perused the pile of wrapped ornaments, a trove of more memories. "I'm so glad that you are home again. I really miss you when you're gone. The exciting trips you get to do all the time. I envy it a little as well. Oh! Here we go!" Iain unwrapped a small dark blue one and unveiled a silvery metal cut out of the Empire State Building attached to a red ribbon.

"New York! Three years ago. That was not a fairy-tale trip! Well some of it was good. Why we just went for a long weekend I can't remember. That was insane the way we kept trying to cram it all in. We just kept on nearly missing things and we barely had time to breathe." He sipped his wine and watched the light reflecting off the ornament as it dangled in his fingers.

"The best and worst bit was that Saturday night. On our way to Greenwich Village from Brooklyn. We were changing trains in the subway from some letter to another letter that I still can't remember. And then there was that kid in torn denim. Looking like a reject from Fame. He called me a faggot. I had gone to look at the map and he must have spotted something I was wearing that he decided was too gay. He came over to me and started shouting about how I wasn't welcome. And then you appeared. He was about to push me and you just materialised by his side and I think that shocked him. The look on his face." Iain chuckled

"You would have thought a ghost had gotten him. And you just turned him around and gave him a telling off, like a schoolteacher! I don't know how you did it, but you didn't shout, you didn't insult him. You just laid it out there. I can't remember it all but there was a bit about how that language isn't appropriate or something like that, how he could be a better person and how the future shouldn't be built on hatred.

And he just stood there. Well at least until he shrugged and disappeared into the next train. You were my knight in shining armour." Adam watched Iain continue to observe the lights dancing on the ornament as it evoked that memory.

"I remember too. I was terrified. After I had my hand on his arm I was convinced he was going to stab me or shot or something. So, I just went for it. I could see the shock and fear on your face and that was something that I wasn't going to allow to happen. I also remember why we only went for a long weekend." Adam sniffed a bit his eyes moist at the memory.

"I had work trips either side and that was all the time we could fit in. I'm sorry. It still feels like that sometimes. We have to cram it all in. It is like life is going on without me. You're going on without me, and I hate that." He used the back of his hand to wipe away the tears that were forming at the corners of this eyes. Iain moved closer and kissed him lightly on the cheek.

"I'll always wait for you silly. Where would I be without you looking out for me?" They kissed briefly, sitting back on their heels each with a hand cupped behind the other's head. Adam with his eyes closed, Iain watching Adam's face intently.

"More wine?" Adam asked coughing to hide his embarrassment at his own shame. He took the empty mugs into the kitchen and got them both a refill. He paused in the doorway of the kitchen;

Iain was sitting there slowly untangling the string of Christmas lights. The sun was beginning to set but it was still enough light to not need the main light on and that would ruin the atmosphere.

"Here you go. That's the last of it, but careful it is still a bit hot." He handed over Iain's mug and carefully lowered himself down to the floor. "I think we are getting too old for this sitting on the floor malarkey."

"Ha. Speak for yourself!" Iain smiled, and the mischievous glint flashed in his eyes.

"Ha, to you too. Okay, my turn." Adam's hand drifted over the remaining parcels, playing memory lane lucky dip. Settling on one, he quickly removed the wrappings.

"Gavin! It's Gavin. Stockholm. Two years ago, next month." He held up the simple woven corn dolly goat that they had christened Gavin. "We went there for your birthday. You wanted to see some Vikings. We had that nice hotel right in the centre. It was freezing. We wandered around so long every day, just seeing everything. But do you know what I really remember about that trip. I fell ill, just a stinking cold, but I felt rotten. And you looked after me. The last two days of the trip, we just stayed in the room and you made sure I was comfy. You even read to me a bit. You said you don't know what you would do without me. I don't know what I would do without you. You must have been so bored!" Adam reached across and squeezed Iain's hand.

"No, it was fine. You needed me and there was plenty to read and watch when you were sleeping it off. And I will confess the sightseeing had given me blisters on my blisters. So a couple of days just looking after you and staying off my feet was a perfect way to end the trip. You old softie." Iain squeezed Adam's hand in return.

"My go!" He grabbed the one instantly recognisable package, a small black box. "You want to talk bored! Now we both know what that's like. The transatlantic cruise to the Caribbean. Six years ago." The box clicked open and inside there was a small glass bauble in which there 'floated' a miniature cruise ship. "Merry Christmas from the S.S. Ursula. That was a devil's deal that we struck taking that holiday." Iain held the faux glass bauble up between them.

"We should have flown there and sailed back." Adam said, Iain nodded his agreement.

"But we learnt our lesson. The hard way. They tried so hard, there was so much going on, but we discovered that we just get really, really, bored stuck in the same place for that long." Iain looked at the tiny model vessel.

"That we did." Adam agreed.

"You know the only thing that made it worth it? We got to spend so much time together and we didn't drive each other crazy. Well, only in the good way." Iain winked at him as he stood and placed the bauble on the tree. He turned back to find Adam had moved and was standing a few paces away having dug out the star from the box.

"We don't do that yet. We've still got the other bits to do first." Iain's face showed his confusion.

"I know, but there is a something I want to say about the star. And we only talk about the other decorations. The ones we both bought. We didn't buy this together, not exactly, you bought it for me. On our first date. At that Christmas Market in the centre of town. Nine years ago yesterday. I used to hate Christmas, it always reminded me of how I had fallen out with my family. Your lot can be a pain, but at least they still talk to you. I've had to build a new family and you're part of that. And because of the travel I've been feeling like my life has been getting in the way of living my life. All this has reminded me that I miss you and that I want to do this with you until we are both definitely too old to sit on the floor for sorting the decorations. Iain Makkary. I love you and would like to spend the rest of my life with you." Adam dropped abruptly to one knee. "Will you marry me?"

Iain's jaw dropped, he crossed the space between them and pulled Adam to his feet.

"Yes I will! You soft sod. I most definitely will!" He pulled him into a huge hug and began laughing happily.

The sun sank low enough to wash their living room with warm golden light, Iain spotted the Mistletoe he had hung earlier just a few paces away. Taking Adam's hand he gently jerked his head and quirked his eyebrows up indicating behind his lover, Adam turned and saw the dangling mistletoe. He smiled in response.

The couple crossed the short distance hand in hand and kissed deeply beneath the mistletoe as the sun made them and the bough over their heads glow golden in the winter sunset.

Afterword

I feel a little like a mystical / literary Prometheus, mistletoe has a long tradition in many cultures and what I am doing here is stealing from the past to reframe that so people can reconnect with the wonder of what has come before.

Each of these stories draws upon those beliefs and through the lives of the fictional residents of Old Bridge and its environs, or their descendants. I hope that you have enjoyed this journey from an uncertain past to a happily mysterious present.

In the darkest times of the year we, as a species, have always felt drawn to find ways to remind ourselves that it will pass. That there is something beyond, be that a spirit that can be summoned after they have died, or the spirit of happiness that can be encouraged to occupy our homes and our hearts.

From Adam Crow and Iain MacDonald's separation to Adam Wynne and Iain Makkary's reconciliation despite the centuries that divide them as characters they are united as part of the universal human experience of seeking love and fearing its loss. For the women who have had to navigate the threat of jealous rivals and the perils of motherhood again the universality of suffering and the desire to push through can hopefully unite us

244

as people to see that hope should be nurtured, especially when we feel most hopeless.

And for the witches and elves that occupy the edges and the outsides of the normal world, we see that help comes where it is needed, and trust comes when it is earned.

So I hope that you, gentle reader, will find your hope, your cheer and your peace now and in the darkest times of your life, be they physical or metaphorical.

Content Warnings

Any story is a journey but you sometimes need to know a little about the destination or the route being taken before you can agree to going on it.

To help those who prefer to know the route before agreeing to the journey here are some quick key themes to help you decide. All of these are works of fiction and utilise elements of 'magic' to a greater or lesser extent and if that is not to your taste, I recommend another book.

- ❖ Prologue: By Balder's Blood
    - ➢ Casual Violence; Deception; Death of a child
- ❖ The Lover's Promise
    - ➢ Grief; Allusions to Domestic Abuse; Historical/religious homophobia
- ❖ The Maiden's Dream
    - ➢ Hints of Domestic abuse; Allusion to homophobic shame
- ❖ The Secret Posey
    - ➢ Bullying; Manipulation / Mind control; Violence / attempted murder
- ❖ The Mother's Prayer
    - ➢ Miscarriage; Childhood illness

- ❖ The Falling Child
  - ➢ Childhood illness; orphan/ grief; Alzheimer's / dementia; historical medical practices
- ❖ The Good Host
  - ➢ Casual abuse/bullying; Nightmare type retribution
- ❖ The Winter Cheer
  - ➢ Grief; Depression; Post-War trauma
- ❖ The Peace Bringer
  - ➢ Drug abuse / drink spiking; homophobic language; Family disputes / estrangement

Printed in Great Britain
by Amazon

19855844R00150